100 Favorite Mysteries of the Century

Selected by the Independent Mystery Booksellers Association

edited by Jim Huang

A Drood Review Book
THE CRUM CREEK PRESS
Carmel, Indiana

Acknowledgments

The editor would like to acknowledge the invaluable assistance of Jeanne Jacobson, Jennie Jacobson, Amy Proni and Beth Thoenen in the preparation of this book.

100 Favorite Mysteries of the Century

ISBN: 0-9625804-6-5

Cover art by Robin Agnew (Aunt Agatha's, Ann Arbor, MI)

First edition: December 2000
Third printing: October 2001

The Crum Creek Press
c/o The Drood Review
484 East Carmel Drive #378
Carmel, IN 46032

www.droodreview.com

We dedicate this book to our many friends in the mystery community, to the wonderful authors — past and present — whose work we love, and to our customers with whom we share this passion.

Contents

Introduction

We'd like to introduce you to one hundred of our best friends.

As booksellers who specialize in mysteries, we offer our customers tens of thousands of titles — whodunits, thrillers, caper novels, espionage tales. We're matchmakers, putting the right books into the hands of the right people. We know everything there is to know about all of these books, if not off the tops of our heads, then through the reference books and other tools we keep close at hand. Looking for something great to read? We stand ready to help.

The Independent Mystery Booksellers Association represents booksellers from all types of businesses wholly or substantially devoted to the sale of mystery books. Some work in traditional stores, some are mail-order dealers and others work off the Internet — many do all three at once. Most of our members sell both new and used books; others specialize in one or the other, or in signed books or first editions for collectors or any number of other special niches.

What we have in common is our love of mysteries, and our eagerness to share this passion with you. The Independent Mystery Booksellers Association's 100 Favorite Mysteries of the Century list represents the accumulated wisdom of the most knowledgeable people in the business. These are the books that we most enjoy, the books that we present to our customers over and over again, and the books that we ourselves return to when we want to visit with cherished friends.

We put together this list in the last quarter of 1999, as part of the end of the century hoopla. As we approach the "real" end of the century on December 31, 2000, we have assembled this book to explain and expand on our choices.

Last fall, we began by asking online IMBA members —

those participating in our daily email list — to nominate their 100 favorite books. Over 700 titles were nominated in this first round. After tallying votes, we engaged in several weeks of lively email discussion in which we reminded each other of favorites, and weighed the merits of various authors and titles. Then we conducted a second round of voting to narrow the list.

The hardest decision that we had to make early on was to limit each author to just one title on the final list. This was especially difficult for authors who write several different kinds of mysteries, and it also proved challenging when we considered some of the more prolific mystery authors. In the end, however, we were for the most part able to rally support for one title by each of these authors. (Though, as you'll see in Part II of this book, not always.) Just as readers like to start series with the first entry, we had a preference — though not a rule — for firsts in series. This is where many of us first discovered these authors, and their fresh voices left lasting impressions.

At this point, there were about 85 titles that had support from a significant number of stores — and still dozens more to compete for the last few slots on the list. I asked Pat Kehde of The Raven Bookstore (Lawrence, Kansas) and Kathleen Riley of Black Bird Mysteries (Keedysville, Maryland) to work with me as a committee to finalize the list based on the votes and other instructions of all participating businesses.

The most surprising aspect of this process, as Kate Birkel of The Mystery Bookstore (Omaha, Nebraska) notes in her comments in Part II, is how much agreement there was among this diverse group of booksellers. To be sure, there were differences of opinion and our email exchanges were sometimes vigorous and impassioned. And at each stage of the process, the narrowing down was agonizingly difficult — even at that first stage where we could each list a whole 100 titles. (100 is not as many as you think.) It was also true that some booksellers viewed the task differently from others, trying to think in terms of "best" in addition to "favorite." Clearly, there's a correlation between the "best mysteries of the century" and "our favorite mysteries of the century." But they are not the same thing.

These differences tended to balance out through the participation of lots and lots of people.

We left off many historically significant titles. There's no question that titles like Mickey Spillane's *I, the Jury* had a major impact on the development of the mystery story — but that was not the criterion that we were using.

It's also worth emphasizing that this is a list of 100 favorite books, and not a list of 100 favorite authors. It's startling to realize that classic writers such as Erle Stanley Gardner and Emma Lathen are missing from this list, as are current favorites such as William Tapply and Archer Mayor. These are just a few examples of great writers who are also models of consistency. None of their titles stand out as a favorite, even as their overall bodies of work would insure their inclusion on an IMBA list of 100 favorite authors.

Since the release of this list at the end of 1999, I've seen two significant criticisms: that as booksellers we are too much influenced by sales figures and that the list is too heavily weighted towards recent titles.

To the first charge, we plead innocent. It's certainly true that sales matter to booksellers, and that we are aware of which titles sell most in our businesses. (IMBA even compiles a monthly bestseller list, which you can find on our website at www.mysterybooksellers.com.) It's also true that there's a strong correlation between our favorites and what we sell — naturally, we recommend our favorites first.

But when you look carefully at the list, you'll see that while there might be a correlation between our favorites list and our bestsellers lists, there are also lots of titles that appear on one list but not the other. I think every mystery bookseller has an author that they'll tell you about with a tinge of heartbreak in their voice, an author they just can't persuade their customers to buy — it's one of those weird intangibles about this business. I'm delighted to see some of these writers recognized here.

Especially with the classics — but even with more contemporary titles that we can already think of as "new" classics — the more important thing to remember is that we discovered many of these books before we started selling books. Indeed, these are the titles that inspired us to become mystery booksellers. If there's any influencing going on here, it's not in the sales figures of the books, but in the qualities of the books themselves — these books truly changed the courses of our lives, as Jane Hooper of Sherlock's Home (Liberty, Missouri) attests in her essay on *Booked to Die.*

To the second charge — that the list is too heavily weighted towards recent titles — we plead guilty. We can't deny that there are only 23 titles from the first half of the twentieth century on our list. There are, however, mitigating circumstances. First, as noted above, we were not trying to produce a list of the most historically significant mysteries. As the most knowledgeable people in the business, we certainly could do so — and it would be a different list from what you have in front of you.

We are mindful of the genre's classics, and we treasure them. At the same time, we know that mysteries have changed over the years. There's a unique — and timeless — pleasure to the most ingenious of the genre's classic mystery denouements. But today's mysteries go beyond the puzzle, and encompass a richness in style, setting and characterization that was rare in the century's early decades. Today's writers are responding to the demands of today's readers, who want to see resolutions every bit as clever as those of the past but also insist that writers meet the highest literary standards. If we are more partial to these newer titles, it's simply that we are readers of our times.

We are delighted with the many ways that talented writers have expanded the boundaries of the mystery story. At the end of one century, when you look at this list of 100 titles, you see just how strong this genre has become, and imagine how much we have to look forward to in the new century.

Jim Huang
Director, Independent Mystery Booksellers Association
Deadly Passions Bookshop, Carmel, IN

Part I

100 Favorite Mysteries of the Century

Arranged chronologically. The year indicated is for the original publication in English, either in Britain or the US.

1900-1909

The Hound of the Baskervilles *by Arthur Conan Doyle* (1902)
The Circular Staircase *by Mary Roberts Rinehart* (1908)

1910-1919

The Thirty-Nine Steps *by John Buchan* (1915)

1920-1929

The Murder of Roger Ackroyd *by Agatha Christie* (1926)

1930-1939

The Maltese Falcon *by Dashiell Hammett* (1930)
The Sands of Windee *by Arthur Upfield* (1931)
Murder Must Advertise *by Dorothy L. Sayers* (1933)
The Postman Always Rings Twice *by James M. Cain* (1934)
The Three Coffins *by John Dickson Carr* (1935)
Hamlet, Revenge *by Michael Innes* (1937)
The Beast Must Die *by Nicholas Blake* (1938)
Rebecca *by Daphne du Maurier* (1938)
Some Buried Caesar *by Rex Stout* (1938)
A Coffin for Dimitrios *by Eric Ambler* (1939)
The Big Sleep *by Raymond Chandler* (1939)

1940-1949

Death of a Peer *by Ngaio Marsh* (1940)
The Wrong Murder *by Craig Rice* (1940)
Green for Danger *by Christianna Brand* (1944)
The Moving Toyshop *by Edmund Crispin* (1946)
The Fabulous Clipjoint *by Fredric Brown* (1947)
I Married a Dead Man *by Cornell Woolrich* (1948)
Cat of Many Tails *by Ellery Queen* (1949)
Brat Farrar *by Josephine Tey* (1949)

1950-1959

Smallbone Deceased *by Michael Gilbert* (1950)
An English Murder *by Cyril Hare* (1951)
The Tiger in the Smoke *by Margery Allingham* (1952)
The Talented Mr. Ripley *by Patricia Highsmith* (1955)
A Dram of Poison *by Charlotte Armstrong* (1956)
The Hours Before Dawn *by Celia Fremlin* (1958)
The List of Adrian Messenger *by Philip MacDonald*
  (1959)

1960-1969

To Kill a Mockingbird *by Harper Lee* (1960)
A Stranger in My Grave *by Margaret Millar* (1960)
The Spy Who Came in from the Cold *by John le Carré*
  (1963)
The Deep Blue Good-by *by John D. MacDonald* (1964)
The Chill *by Ross Macdonald* (1964)
In the Heat of the Night *by John Ball* (1965)
Cotton Comes to Harlem *by Chester Himes* (1965)

1970-1979

Time and Again *by Jack Finney* (1970)
The Laughing Policeman *by Maj Sjöwall & Per Wahlöö*
  (1970)
No More Dying Then *by Ruth Rendell* (1971)

An Unsuitable Job for a Woman *by P.D. James* (1972)
Sadie When She Died *by Ed McBain* (1972)
Dark Nantucket Noon *by Jane Langton* (1975)
Crocodile on the Sandbank *by Elizabeth Peters* (1975)
The Sunday Hangman *by James McClure* (1977)
Edwin of the Iron Shoes *by Marcia Muller* (1977)
The Last Good Kiss *by James Crumley* (1978)
Chinaman's Chance *by Ross Thomas* (1978)
Whip Hand *by Dick Francis* (1979)
One Corpse Too Many *by Ellis Peters* (1979)

1980-1989

Looking for Rachel Wallace *by Robert B. Parker* (1980)
Thus Was Adonis Murdered *by Sarah Caudwell* (1981)
The Man With a Load of Mischief *by Martha Grimes*
    (1981)
Death by Sheer Torture *by Robert Barnard* (1982)
The Man Who Liked Slow Tomatoes *by K.C. Constantine*
    (1982)
"A" Is For Alibi *by Sue Grafton* (1982)
The Thin Woman *by Dorothy Cannell* (1984)
Deadlock *by Sara Paretsky* (1984)
Strike Three You're Dead *by R.D. Rosen* (1984)
When the Bough Breaks *by Jonathan Kellerman* (1985)
Sleeping Dog *by Dick Lochte* (1985)
When the Sacred Ginmill Closes *by Lawrence Block*
    (1986)
Tourist Season *by Carl Hiaasen* (1986)
The Ritual Bath *by Faye Kellerman* (1986)
Rough Cider *by Peter Lovesey* (1986)
The Monkey's Raincoat *by Robert Crais* (1987)
Old Bones *by Aaron Elkins* (1987)
The Killings at Badger's Drift *by Caroline Graham* (1987)
Presumed Innocent *by Scott Turow* (1987)
A Great Deliverance *by Elizabeth George* (1988)
The Silence of the Lambs *by Thomas Harris* (1988)

A Thief of Time *by Tony Hillerman* (1988)
Death's Bright Angel *by Janet Neel* (1988)
Black Cherry Blues *by James Lee Burke* (1989)

1990-1999

Get Shorty *by Elmore Leonard* (1990)
If Ever I Return, Pretty Peggy-O *by Sharyn McCrumb*
  (1990)
Devil in a Blue Dress *by Walter Mosley* (1990)
Sanibel Flats *by Randy Wayne White* (1990)
Aunt Dimity's Death *by Nancy Atherton* (1992)
Booked to Die *by John Dunning* (1992)
Bootlegger's Daughter *by Margaret Maron* (1992)
The Ice House *by Minette Walters* (1992)
Track of the Cat *by Nevada Barr* (1993)
The Beekeeper's Apprentice *by Laurie R. King* (1993)
Child of Silence *by Abigail Padgett* (1993)
The Concrete Blonde *by Michael Connelly* (1994)
The Yellow Room Conspiracy *by Peter Dickinson* (1994)
One for the Money *by Janet Evanovich* (1994)
Mallory's Oracle *by Carol O'Connell* (1994)
A Broken Vessel *by Kate Ross* (1994)
Who in Hell Is Wanda Fuca? *by G.M. Ford* (1995)
Vanishing Act *by Thomas Perry* (1995)
Blue Lonesome *by Bill Pronzini* (1995)
Concourse *by S.J. Rozan* (1995)
Darkness, Take My Hand *by Dennis Lehane* (1996)
The Club Dumas *by Arturo Perez-Reverte* (1996)
A Test of Wills *by Charles Todd* (1996)
Dreaming of the Bones *by Deborah Crombie* (1997)
Blood at the Root *by Peter Robinson* (1997)
On Beulah Height *by Reginald Hill* (1998)

100 Favorite Mysteries of the Century

Essays in this section have been contributed by booksellers from Independent Mystery Booksellers Association member businesses, reflecting their individual tastes and opinions. You'll find complete information about these businesses in Part III of this book, beginning on page 143.

These essays are arranged alphabetically by author. The year indicated is for the original publication either in Britain or the United States; alternate titles are listed where applicable.

The Tiger in the Smoke by Margery Allingham (1952)

If I had to choose just one mystery novel to take with me to that proverbial desert island, I wouldn't have to think twice, especially since Margery Allingham is, hands down, my very favorite writer. In an oeuvre that is notable for its originality in many respects, *The Tiger in the Smoke* is truly Allingham's masterpiece, though I am also extremely fond of *More Work for the Undertaker* and *Police at the Funeral* (the latter of which does a marvelous job of turning some mystery conventions completely on their heads).

For me, however, this one has it all: humor, pathos, drama, suspense and atmosphere. The plot seems deceptively simple. A conscienceless killer (a cliché in today's mystery market) is loose in London (known as "the Smoke"). Where will Jack Havoc choose to strike next? Can Scotland Yard cage the Tiger before he terrorizes the entire city? That all seems straightforward enough. The stage is set for a race-against-time, can-they-catch-him-fast-enough generic thriller. But in the hands of a master like Allingham, nothing is generic, because the characters who inhabit her world step beyond convention. Canon Avril, a saintly churchman who is Albert Campion's uncle, bears a guilty secret, one which makes him peculiarly vulnerable to the demon known as Jack Havoc. The canon appears to be the epitome of pure Goodness, with Havoc as his antithesis.

Do pure Evil and pure Goodness exist?

Allingham weaves a stunning morality play around this question, and along the way to her answer, the reader will alternately shiver and laugh at the ridiculousness of evil and applaud and bemoan the culpability of goodness.

Dean James
Murder by the Book, Houston, TX

A Coffin for Dimitrios by Eric Ambler (1939) (aka A Mask for Dimitrios)

Mr. Latimer is the quintessential naïve amateur caught up in the tangled alliances and antagonisms of pre-World War II Europe. The story begins in Turkey then moves to other countries of central Europe, including the Balkans, ending in Paris. These are perfect locations for this espionage-noir novel. Their long history of bloody vengeance and double-dealing provides a perfect setting for Mr. Latimer, a former school teacher and now a successful writer of murder mysteries who is led like a lamb to slaughter in the murky world of Eric Ambler's Europe.

I love this book, partly for the fascinating plot, which seems so straightforward and grows so complex. But mostly I love it for the sense of place and the moody, ironic tone. Who else but Ambler can create those dark, dirty, damp streets of Balkan cities, or packed trains moving in and out of crumbling, provincial yet menacing places? This author established the genre of the lonely little guy caught in international intrigue and he's still the best.

Pat Kehde
The Raven Bookstore, Lawrence, KS

A Dram of Poison by Charlotte Armstrong (1956)

Charlotte Armstrong was one of the best known and most

prolific American female mystery writers in the 1950s. She was frequently an Edgar nominee and won in 1956 for *A Dram of Poison*. At a time when hardboiled private PIs were assuming the mantle of the American mystery, Armstrong wrote about evils and horrors visited on ordinary people who led decent lives — far removed from the decadent side of society — and the strengths they drew on to respond to their misfortunes.

A Dram of Poison is about a mouse of a man who has fallen in love with a woman he married for convenience. He is now miserable because his bossy sister has convinced him, through authoritative psychological insight, that his wife could not possibly return his affection. Deciding to take his life, he steals some poison — putting it in a salad dressing bottle to take home. But he misplaces the bottle!

Most of the book revolves around a growing hodgepodge of odd, apparently stereotypic characters, trying to help him find the poison before it is too late. These people are expertly and efficiently drawn and they are vivid to me *years* after having read the book. Ambitiously, Armstrong has this growing brood of hunters (a bus driver, a nurse he's had his eye on, a civic minded wealthy woman and a randy artist, for starters) pile in the car, while also having a spirited discussion of free will vs. determinism. This discussion gets a little tedious and at times feels a little forced, especially when you know that someone might make a salad at any moment! The generally provocative discussion between people who don't conform to type lulls you into forgetting how tense you are getting.

I was delightedly surprised and satisfied by the ending.

Kate Mattes
Kate's Mystery Books, Cambridge, MA

Aunt Dimity's Death by Nancy Atherton (1992)

When I learned of Aunt Dimity's death, I was stunned. Not because she was dead, but because I had never known she'd been alive.

Lori Shepherd, a young woman down on her luck, receives a mysterious letter regarding a potential inheritance from Dimity Westwood, "Aunt Dimity." Lori's shock is due to the fact that Aunt Dimity was a make-believe character her mother used to tell adventure stories about at bedtime. Or at least Lori thought she was make-believe. Now Lori is on her way to England to inherit Aunt Dimity's estate. As in all good mysteries, there is a catch to the inheritance. Lori must discover the secret hidden among hundreds of letters in Aunt Dimity's cottage. Much to Lori's surprise, the letters are correspondence with her own mother.

Lori is not without help along the way. There is her faithful childhood companion Reginald, a pink stuffed rabbit; Bill Willis of the law firm handling the estate; and Aunt Dimity herself, as a ghost. Through a journal in the den of the cottage Aunt Dimity leaves cryptic messages for Lori. These clues lead Lori, Bill and Reginald on quite an adventure before the mystery is solved.

Aunt Dimity's Death is the first in a series by Nancy Atherton. It is a cozy lover's heaven. It is a heartwarming, charming, funny and delightful book. Atherton wraps Aunt Dimity's gentle heart around you as you read. Soon Dimity and Reginald are as much a part of the story as Lori and Bill. This book is best read with a cup of tea, a biscuit or two and a warm fire. You will definitely smile at the end of the story — then reach for the second book and another cup of tea.

Yvonne Peaslee
Murder, Mystery & Mayhem, Farmington, MI

In the Heat of the Night by John Ball (1965)

In the Heat of the Night is John Ball's gripping first novel. Introducing homicide detective Virgil Tibbs, the hero of several subsequent books, *In the Heat of the Night* was made into a film starring Sidney Poitier and Rod Steiger, and formed the basis of a television series featuring Carroll O'Connor.

The Carolina town of Wells is sweltering in the August heat, oppressive even late at night. Officer Sam Wood, patrolling the town in his squad car, has found everything in order until he discovers a body in the middle of the highway. The victim is Maestro Enrico Mantoli, a conductor brought to town to organize a music festival intended to "put Wells on the map" and bring in some tourist dollars. Both Sam Wood and Police Chief Bill Gillespie, new on the job and totally untrained for his new responsibilities, are poorly equipped to solve a murder.

When Sam Wood is sent to the railway station to look for suspicious characters, he thinks the black man he finds there may be the perpetrator. Virgil Tibbs, passing through town after visiting his mother, is a respected investigator in Pasadena. After Tibbs is vouched for by his California superior, Wood and Gillespie would like to send him on his way, but George Endicott, patron of the music festival and Mantoli's host, insists that Tibbs help the local force to investigate the murder.

The prejudice of the small Southern town — not only against African Americans but against Italians and other outsiders — is well-detailed by Ball. To their own amazement, Wood and Gillespie begin to respect Tibbs and his abilities. A good detective, fine local color and strong characters make *In the Heat of the Night* an outstanding crime novel which won an Edgar Award from the Mystery Writers of America and a Gold Dagger from the British Crime Writers Association.

Mary Helen Becker
Booked for Murder, Madison, WI

Death by Sheer Torture by Robert Barnard (1982) (aka Sheer Torture)

If Evelyn Waugh had written detective stories, he might have produced something very like *Death by Sheer Torture*, a marvelous piece of social satire set in the country home of a cracked aristocratic family that may well remind you of the Mitfords or the Sitwells. Blessed with more money than talent, the Trethowan family members naturally turn to the arts for self-fulfillment when they aren't flirting with Nazis or figuratively and literally trying to stab each other in the back.

When the family patriarch is found dead in spangled tights, strangled by his own sexual torture device, it could be an accident, but Scotland Yard suspects foul play and assigns to the case the only person on the force capable of understanding the family dynamics. Perry Trethowan, the family white sheep and gratefully estranged son of the dead man, isn't a bit pleased to return home, although he wouldn't be a bit surprised to learn that one of his siblings or cousins had done the old man in.

Satire is often more mean-spirited than funny, but Barnard manages to skewer the upper classes here and in the equally hilarious *Corpse in a Gilded Cage* with the same high wit he employed to lampoon academia in *Death of an Old Goat* or the literary world in *Death of a Mystery Writer.* An unabashed left-winger who always seems genuinely happy to meet fans, Barnard is the grand master of the five p's of mystery writing: "people, plot, pace, place and the knack of turning the graceful phrase."

Tom & Enid Schantz
Rue Morgue, Boulder, CO

Track of the Cat by Nevada Barr (1993)

Back in 1994, my wife and I decided to start a science fiction and mystery bookstore. *Track of the Cat* was one of the reasons why.

That's not just because it's a good read. This was a watershed book for Deb.

Much of her previous reading was "the old classics" — English drawing room mysteries and light cozies. It was fun stuff, but too artificial, too perfect. Even private eyes like Kinsey Millhone seemed to be sealed off in their own little world.

Anna Pigeon isn't like that. She leaps off the first pages of

Track of the Cat as a real person. She is curmudgeonly, introverted, a woman who gets tired and thirsty and angry. To use Nevada Barr's words in a slightly different context, the earth is hers with no taint of heaven.

I might get thumped for saying this, but Anna Pigeon is a lot like my wife. I think Deb realized this when she read the book, and that it made the mystery genre come alive for her in a new way. She connected herself to Anna. We've sold a lot of Nevada Barr books because she can express that connection, and we've learned to look for books that forge that kind of bond with us. It's what really excites us about mysteries.

Anna doesn't appeal just to us. *Track of the Cat* was an immediate sensation when it was published — it won the Agatha and Anthony Awards for the year, and you'd better be ready to sell some body parts if you want a first edition.

Some of the credit goes to Barr's magnificent landscape writing — she loves the natural world, and she has a gift for letting you see it through her eyes. But most of it was Anna. She was one of the first woman detectives with the authority of a law enforcement officer but a life of her own to live, and that gives her a vibrancy and complexity that's rare in any fiction.

Chris Aylott & Deb Tomaselli
Space-Crime Continuum, Northampton, MA

The Beast Must Die by Nicholas Blake (1938)

"It is surprising how entirely reconciled I am to the idea that, within a few days (weather permitting), I shall commit a murder." So says Frank Cairnes about half way through this wonderful crime novel that may or may not be in the style of the classic "inverted" story. Cairnes had a son — Martie — who was killed in a hit and run accident. This information is provided on page one of the novel so it is not giving anything away to say that revenge is at the heart of this tale.

The police have come up against stone walls and have no leads to follow so Cairnes takes on the task of finding the person responsible for his son's death. The author constructs a very clever and entirely believable scenario with seemingly unrelated bits of information and a few logical deductions along with a small leap of faith that leads him to the man he believes responsible for his son's murder. Cairnes befriends this man, moves into his home and plots his revenge.

The book is written in multiple points of view and the detective, Nigel Strangeways, is not even introduced until half way into the book. It is all but guaranteed you will think you have it all sorted out — and all but guaranteed you will be wrong. A completely delightful read.

The author, whose real name was C. Day Lewis, was Poet Laureate of England (1968). The character of Strangeways is featured in sixteen of the author's twenty novels.

Bruce Taylor
San Francisco Mystery Bookstore, San Francisco, CA

When the Sacred Ginmill Closes by Lawrence Block (1986)

Larry Block is a master storyteller both with novels and short stories, writing several series and winning major awards — the Edgar, the Anthony, the Shamus — some more than once. He's the recipient of a Grand Master Award from Mystery Writers of America.

When the Sacred Ginmill Closes is greatly expanded from Block's Edgar-winning short story, "By The Dawn's Early Light." The endings of the two are the same and I must not tell you that ending here because it will spoil the book for you but if you haven't read it — beg, borrow or steal a copy from your best pal and read it asap.

It's 1975 in New York City and ex-cop, unlicensed private-eye Matthew Scudder is doing favors for his friends. His friends are his drinking buddies from the bars, the taverns, the ginmills and saloons not too far from his room at a west side hotel. Skip Devoe's tax records are missing and Scudder has to get them back. Tommy Tillary's wife is dead and Scudder has to clear him. Tim Pat's after-hours joint was robbed and Scudder has to find out who did it. Drinking steadily, Scudder somehow accomplishes all of the above by sheer doggedness while his investigation and cop's intuition lead to a stunning climax.

From this book forward, I believe Scudder has a tougher edge and along the way he finds the will and courage to give up the alcohol. In doing so, he becomes more human. Maybe it's only the author stretching and growing, but it translates into his books just getting better. As readers we can hardly wait for the next release.

Jan Grape
Mysteries & More Online, Austin, TX

Green for Danger by Christianna Brand (1944)

Set in a hospital in the English countryside during World War II, this short novel at first appears to be simply a variation on the country-house murder with the coloration of the times (e.g. air raids) added for emphasis. The classic "closed community" is that of the staff of the hospital and much of the plot revolves upon how the secrets of their "other " (read "pre-war") lives color their current experiences.

After an air raid, several wounded men are brought in for treatment. One is an elderly man, at first unidentified but later found to be the village postman. He dies on the operating table during fairly routine procedures; an inspector is sent to investigate and soon finds that this was murder. Inspector Cockrill is Christianna Brand's main series figure, and at times in this novel seems to be *almost* incidental. He is an unassuming, quiet, gentle man who has known many of the people involved for many years, and he maneuvers (or hovers) around the periphery for most of the story, rarely taking center stage until the denouement, quite close to the end.

Each suspect is offered up in turn, subtly and carefully, with telling bits and pieces abounding throughout the story. All the characters are fleshed out with care and tenderness by a writer who seems to understand that flawed people are lovable too. Romance, blackmail, comradeship, hatred, love, and peculiar behavior are scattered throughout this well-crafted exercise in classic British mystery. Slow and atmospheric at first while accustoming us to its surroundings, the ending is slam-bang and twisty enough to satisfy anyone with a taste for double-takes.

It's a real pity that Brand wrote so few mystery novels, and a real joy that this one was made into a classic film (1946) worthy of its source. The movie is very good and worth a look; the book is even better!

AbiGail Hamilton
Black Bird Mysteries, Keedysville, MD

The Fabulous Clipjoint by Fredric Brown (1947)

For me, this book is a welter of contrasts that combined to form a completely satisfying whole: a hardboiled detective mystery cut from pure pulp cloth which still manages to have characters that can be caring and supportive of each other. The dangerous, grimy streets of Depression-era Chicago let you almost feel the humid summer heat; the overall impression left is of a vigorous city full of wonder.

Ed Hunter is a young man whose father has just been killed in a back-alley mugging. His Uncle Am brings with him the background glitz and tarnish of the carny when he comes to Chicago to determine if his brother Wally's death was as unplanned as it looked. Between them they encounter crooked cops, honorable pressmen, a gorgeous gun moll and a variety of low life bruisers. With guts and wits, they slowly work through many conflicting possibilities to uncover the plan behind the murder, and the puppetmaster who set it up.

The one discordant note to the book was the lack of development of female characters, every one of whom was self-centered to a fault and almost implausibly one dimensional. The well-rounded and varied male characters more than made up for this, but it seemed another odd contrast.

Early in his career Fredric Brown was known for his science fiction as much as his mysteries, writing dozens of stories in magazines such as *Astounding, Weird Tales* and *Startling Stories* as well as in great mystery pulps such as *Detective Story, Black Mask* and *Thrilling Detective. The Fabulous Clipjoint* won him the Edgar Award for Best First Novel for 1947. Altogether Brown wrote seven novels about the detective team of Ed and Am Hunter, including his last full novel *Mrs. Murphy's Underpants* in 1963.

Alice Bentley
The Stars Our Destination, Evanston, IL

The Thirty-Nine Steps by John Buchan (1915)

The Thirty-Nine Steps takes place in 1914, just before the outbreak of World War I. Richard Hannay, hero of several of Buchan's books, has been in the "Old Country" for three weeks, and is bored after his active and adventurous life in South Africa. After too many tea parties with Imperialist ladies and meetings with New Zealand schoolmasters, he is disillusioned with England, which had always been a sort of Arabian Nights fantasy for him. He resolves to give it one more day or he is back to the Cape.

That very night, he is accosted by an American he recognizes as the occupant of another flat in his building. Hannay takes him in and agrees to listen to his story, which proves to be a tale of intrigue and conspiracy involving most of the countries of Europe and threatening the security of England. When Scudder, Hannay's mysterious visitor, is stabbed to death, Hannay escapes by a clever ruse and decides to head for Scotland where he can use his skills developed on the African veldt to elude his pursuers, both the police — who believe him to be Scudder's killer — and the foreign agents. Hannay's adventures in Scotland include stealing the conspirators' car, disguising himself as a road builder, and using his knowledge of explosives gained through his work in Africa as a mining engineer.

John Buchan, Baron Tweedsmuir (1875-1940), had a distinguished career which is as interesting as those of his heroes. At Brasenose College, Oxford, he was President of the Union and winner of the Newdigate Prize. Called to the bar in 1901, he worked as private secretary for the high commissioner for South Africa, served in Parliament, and was Governor-General of Canada from 1935 to 1940. Though a fine writer who published voluminously, he considered himself an amateur novelist whose true career was politics.

The Thirty-Nine Steps is a wonderful adventure. Made into a film by Alfred Hitchcock in 1935, it has influenced writers of spy novels ever since. If *The Riddle of the Sands* by Erskine Childers (1903) is the first of the great English espionage novels, *The Thirty-Nine Steps* is the second — a classic spy story that is as enjoyable today as it has been for nearly a century.

Mary Helen Becker
Booked for Murder, Madison, WI

Black Cherry Blues by James Lee Burke (1989)

Mention of James Lee Burke's series featuring Louisiana detective and former police officer David Robicheaux instantly evokes the vivid images of the external landscape. Burke is passionate about the flora, fauna and people of the South, and it shows in every carefully chosen phrase. However, he invests just as much consideration in his descriptions of Robicheaux and his internal landscape. Robicheaux may be a deeply flawed character, but he excels in his efforts to better himself and to see things through on the path to justice, however many obstacles he may encounter along the way.

He carries this internal landscape with him in *Black Cherry Blues*, which won the 1989 Edgar for Best Novel, as he takes a break from Louisiana and journeys to Montana. The Vietnam veteran and struggling alcoholic unsuccessfully tries to leave his sorrows over the death of his father and murder of his wife behind, and take his young daughter to a safer place. Burke's novels often are not whodunits, or even whydunits — generally they are more "how-is-Robicheaux-going-to-convince-the-bad-guys-to-stop-its." In this case, the bad guys include the Mafia and oil concerns at odds with the residents of tribal lands.

Pulitzer Prize nominee Burke's greatest attribute lies in his ability to make his readers feel emotions strongly, whether it's distress at the violence Robicheaux and other characters engage in, or the appreciation of a simple meal on the dock of his fish-and-tackle shop with his loved ones, or an acknowledgment of the powers that shape our world.

Maryelizabeth Hart
Mysterious Galaxy, San Diego, CA

The Postman Always Rings Twice by James M. Cain (1934)

I can only imagine the sensation *The Postman Always Rings Twice* created in 1934, because it is still shocking today. In a brief 120 pages, James M. Cain lays out a narrative that is so compelling and so memorable that bits of it will probably stay with you forever.

This is a novel about desire, and the awful twisted paths it takes in the lives of three people — Cora, the beautiful wife; her husband, "The Greek;" and the narrator, Frank, Cora's lover and Nick the Greek's killer. From the second Frank sees Cora, he knows he's hooked. At the most shocking turn of the plot, as Nick lies dead in the car, Frank and Cora make love:

Next thing I knew, I was down there with her, and we were staring into each other's eyes, and locked in each other's arms, and straining to get closer. Hell could have opened for me then, and it wouldn't have made any difference. I had to have her..."

If the two themes of great novels are sex and money, this one has been honed down to the sex only; the money, when it comes, is beside the point.

What sets *Postman* even farther above many other novels in this particular genre is the fact that while it has this raging plot full of passion, it also has one of the cleverest trial scams you'll ever read. It's a virtual model for many other books, and reading it here again, it still seems fresh, because it's so full of twists.

And what does the reader take away from this novel? What path is there to choose through life — the slow, careful and prudent path, taken by the Greek, or the lust-crazed path taken by Frank and Cora? And what of love? The love Frank and Cora profess for each other is like a destructive tornado, poisoned by their actions. Towards the end of the book, Frank says to Cora: "There's nobody else. I love you, Cora. But love, when you get fear in it, it's not love any more. It's hate." Remorse isn't really a part of Frank and Cora's landscape; their easy betrayal of each other is what comes between them. And it blows everything else apart.

Robin Agnew
Aunt Agatha's, Ann Arbor, MI

The Thin Woman by Dorothy Cannell (1984)

Ellie Simons has a problem. She has been invited to a family reunion where she will be forced to spend a weekend in the company of her beautiful and thin cousin Vanessa, thin being the operative word. You see, Ellie's problem is that she is a fat spinster with no marital prospects, fat and no prospects being the operative words. Never mind that she is a successful London decorator and entirely self supporting. In the eyes of her relatives, Ellie is a failure. Then Ellie sees an advertisement for an escort service, and hires Bentley T. Haskell to impersonate her fiancé. Unfortunately, though, what Ellie believes to be an elegant solution to a messy problem merely opens the floodgates to a whole host of other problems, including several attempts on her life.

The Thin Woman masquerades as a cozy, and it succeeds very well at that. It's humorous, the language is not going to offend your sainted grandmother, the physical violence is kept to a minimum and there is no graphic sex. But under that genial cover, the book deals with two very serious issues: emotional abuse and society's condemnation of fat people.

The Thin Woman is the first in a series, and the best of the lot. Cannell was able to sustain the genial nuttiness of this first book over the next three or four books in the series, then started losing her grip, which is a shame. Let's all hope Cannell soon gets her second wind.

Kate Birkel
The Mystery Bookstore, Omaha, NE

The Three Coffins by John Dickson Carr (1935) (aka The Hollow Man)

When Professor Charles Grimaud is shot in his locked study, Dr. Gideon Fell, John Dickson Carr's large, loud and boisterous detective, has found a match for his analytical skills. There are no footsteps in the snow leading to the front stoop of the house, nor is the snow disturbed on the windowsill of the study. All the occupants of Grimaud's house are either accounted for or have been locked into the downstairs sitting room — and the door to the study has been under the close observation of his secretary throughout the critical moments.

Dr. Fell sets about interviewing the inhabitants of the house, including the secretary, whom, we are told at the outset, tells the exact truth of what he sees. In fact, it is this that sets Carr's novels apart — his insistence on stepping outside the four corners of the novel to speak directly to the reader of what can and cannot be relied on.

The Three Coffins is the quintessential example of what Dr. Fell calls the problem of the "hermetically sealed chamber." It offers Dr. Fell's famous digression about how locked room murders can be committed, including his suggestion to the reader to skip the chapter if so inclined. Dr. Fell maintains that mystery stories are a series of improbable solutions to prob-

28

lems, and the reader really doesn't want a solution that is anything less than fabulous. To follow on from a similar discourse of Sherlock Holmes, Dr. Fell is saying that the improbable has to be the actual answer when it is either that or the impossible.

John Dickson Carr was one of the earliest members, the only American member, of the Detection Club founded by G.K. Chesterton and Dorothy L. Sayers. The club had rules about how a mystery had to be written and resolved. Carr's books reflect his adherence to these tenets, perhaps contributing to a tendency of his novels to seem stilted, even dated, by today's standards. But they are among the very best of the classic English mystery novels, proposing wonderful problems that must be solved logically and sequentially to arrive at the final (improbable) solution.

Kathy Phillips
Spenser's Mystery Bookshop, Boston, MA

Thus Was Adonis Murdered by Sarah Caudwell (1981)

Sarah Caudwell (1939-2000) died far too young and left a literary output that was far too meager. She died of cancer and we, her fans, were heartbroken. She wrote four novels only, but what gems they are, each and every one.

Thus Was Adonis Murdered was published in 1981 by Collins in the UK and Scribners in the US. In this novel we are introduced to Hilary Tamar, an Oxford professor who narrates the adventures of a small gang of lunatics, clever young lawyers all, that provide such elegant fun for all those who are prepared to spend the time and attention required. In Caudwell's obituary *(The New York Times,* Feb. 6, 2000), Marilyn Stasio said "although the story revolved around the lusty antics of 'a decorative little group' of junior barristers, it was the classical erudition and acerbic tongue of the narrator, whose sex is never stated, that set the droll tone of the series."

One of the bunch, Julia Larwood, is brilliant in her knowledge of tax laws but hopeless with the day to day complexities of life. She is looking forward to a few days of rest and relaxation in Venice, and perhaps an adonis or two to share her bed, only to end up in jail accused of the murder of one such adonis. Her friends to the rescue. If you only read one book this year, make it this one.

The Shortest Way to Hades (1985), *The Sirens Sang of Murder* (1989) and *The Sibyl in Her Grave* (published posthumously in June 2000) round out the author's output and the adventures of our ragtag bunch.

J.D. Singh
Sleuth of Baker Street, Toronto, Canada

The Big Sleep by Raymond Chandler (1939)

It was about eleven o'clock in the morning, mid-October, with the sun not shining and the look of hard wet rain in the clearness of the foothills.... I was neat, clean, shaved and sober, and I didn't care who knew it. I was everything the well-dressed private detective ought to be. I was calling on four million dollars.

For every cliché hardboiled one-liner you've ever heard, it all starts right here. This is the first of the Philip Marlowe private investigator stories so even if you've seen the movie a hundred times, the original text still bears reading. After 60 years of spin-offs and copycats, Raymond Chandler's Philip Marlowe is still fresh and smart on the page. All of the favorites are here: the dim-witted bombshell blonde, the calculating knockout brunette, the slimy underworld cronies, and the rakish tilt of the fedora on Marlowe's head. Chandler opens us up to a wholly different Los Angeles, one from a different time with a different set of criminals. As much as some things are bound to change, there are some things that have dared to stay the same. The darker side of the city rings true even now in the twenty-first century, with its dark seamy corners where the rabble of life wallows and lurks. If you have ever enjoyed a PI movie or story, you cannot stand to miss the real thing.

Because it is a Chandler novel, the writing is characteristically short and direct. Sentences never run on with endless description, yet Chandler manages to convey a sense of time and place with even the briefest of statements. A strong yet breezy read, this book works for every instance, from the bathtub to the airport and the beach or even while waiting for the doctor in that breezy paper gown, where I seem to get a surprising amount of reading done.

Ann Saunders
Murder, Mystery & Mayhem, Farmington, MI

The Murder of Roger Ackroyd by Agatha Christie (1926)

It is difficult for us nowadays to comprehend the sensation this novel caused when it was first published. When *The Murder of Roger Ackroyd* was published the conventions for Golden Age mystery stories that we now smile about (for their naïveté) were just being formulated. A writer who flouts the rules is commonplace in our time but in England in the 1920s was generally thought of as probably not having the talent to write "a proper mystery." Christie had both the talent and the audacity. Up until that time no one had, I believe, effectively used the twist that Christie employed. If she wasn't the first to use this device, she was certainly the most gifted.

Ackroyd used many of the usual plot elements from 1920s mysteries — village setting, mistaken identities, local squire whom no one likes and many hate, young lovers and mixed alliances, nosy spinsters, the "great detective" in retirement. What made this book sensational is that the story is written from the viewpoint of a country doctor and longtime resident of the village, and thereby doubly or triply seen to be trustworthy. Christie flouted many conventions; she was on dangerous ground and could have been shunned by readers if the book wasn't of such good quality.

Therein lies the crux. *The Murder of Roger Ackroyd* succeeded in the 1920s because it had a sensational premise and was superbly executed. Even though the main twist of the story is now well known, it still succeeds as a well-written story, and a reminder of, and transportation to, another place and time.

AbiGail Hamilton
Black Bird Mysteries, Keedysville, MD

The Concrete Blonde by Michael Connelly (1994)

One summer evening, LAPD homicide detective Harry Bosch, acting on a tip from a prostitute, alone and without calling for backup, kicked down an apartment door and yelled to the man rising from the bed within to freeze. Instead of complying, the man reached under the pillow, and Harry shot him in the chest. As he cuffed the dying man, Harry looked under the pillow for the man's gun and found only a toupee.

It is now four years later, and Harry is being sued by the man's widow for wrongfully causing his death. Despite the testimony that this man was an upstanding member of the community, Harry still believes that he was the serial killer known as the Dollmaker and that this was a "good" shooting. Or at least he did believe it until the cops receive an anonymous note from someone claiming to be the Dollmaker; a new body is unearthed, one killed years after Harry had kicked down the door; and the trial reveals that the deceased had a videotaped alibi for one of the shootings.

Connelly is at his best in this, his third novel. He captures the flavor of LA in the time AK (after Rodney King) when no one trusts the police, not even the city attorney who is defending Harry. He skillfully describes Harry's retreat into himself and away from his friends and other cops while the trial inexorably moves towards a verdict which could doom his career. As inside sources leak information to the press and to the plaintiff's attorney, Harry continues his investigation through the dark lonely streets of LA when he realizes that there may indeed be another serial killer at work and that it may even be one of his fellow officers. This is high drama, artfully constructed by a master storyteller.

Joe Morales
Capital Crimes Mystery Bookstore, Sacramento, CA

The Man Who Liked Slow Tomatoes by K.C. Constantine (1982)

The Man Who Liked Slow Tomatoes is the fifth entry in a series featuring Mario Balzic, chief of police of Rocksburg, Pennsylvania. Rocksburg is a small city somewhere in the western coal mining regions of the state, suffering from the slump in the coal mining industry.

Mario is asked to find a laid-off miner. The missing man will not search for other employment; he feels emasculated by welfare, food stamps and his wife's minimum wage job, and beats her as a result. He is also under surveillance by the state narcotics cops. His wife turns out to be the daughter of a man who was a unionist along with Mario's father. The old man still lives two doors away from his daughter and Balzic feels guilty that he hasn't visited him since his own father died.

Mario's life is complicated by contract negotiations for the police department. As police chief, he is in management, but his sympathies lie with his staff who are underpaid and over-worked. He has little sympathy for slick and not-so-slick politicians, but recognizes that they can't give much in the negotiations because of the depressed economy of the time.

The Man Who Liked Slow Tomatoes is a fine entry in this true-to-life series about a sensitive man in a difficult job. Constantine's characters are finely developed over the series. Our hero Mario Balzic is caring, resourceful, tough when he has to be, a loving family man who drinks a little too much and doesn't always sleep well. He is the kind of policeman that we could use a lot more of and he gets the job done with a minimum of damage to the lives of those affected by crime. The series is realistic in the same manner that Georges Simenon's Maigret or Joseph Hansen's Dave Brandstetter series are, and Balzic is a similar kind of detective.

John Leininger
Grave Matters, Cincinnati, OH

The Monkey's Raincoat by Robert Crais (1987)

There are plenty of contemporary private eye novels with gaudy protagonists full of peculiar quirks or "unique" traits. It's worth noting right at the start that Robert Crais' detective, Elvis Cole, is a well-adjusted white male with a positive attitude who lives a solitary and simple life. He wisecracks with the best of them — parts of this book are very funny — and he's as tough as they come, but he's as normal as anyone you'll encounter in a regular day, unlike many of today's private eyes.

If what's remarkable about Cole is that he's so unremarkable, the same can't be said for the way Crais portrays his client. And that, I believe, is why *The Monkey's Raincoat* stood out so emphatically when it was first published, and why Crais endures as a leading practitioner of the private eye subgenre. Cole's client, Ellen Lang, has a simple problem: her husband and her son are missing. Ellen's friend Janet has urged her to seek help — dragging her into Cole's office and trying to do the talking for her. Mort Lang was a lousy husband, but he's all that Ellen has. And that's the real problem: Mort's left Ellen completely lacking in self-esteem and so dependent that she doesn't even know how to write a check. The plot follows a conventional and straightforward outline, so it's no surprise when Mort's found dead.

Cole doggedly pursues the case, but it's even more important that he and his partner, Joe Pike, find a way to give Ellen her life back. In this current era of the private eye as social worker, Crais is unsurpassed at portraying this process; he does it deftly with few, but effective, strokes. If we know all along where the story's going, it's nevertheless suspenseful because

Crais is such a great writer. The story sticks with us because we all hope that we will respond to a crisis as well as Ellen Lang does, and we all hope that when we look for help, it'll be as stout, effective, tenacious and devoted as Elvis Cole.

Jim Huang
Deadly Passions Bookshop, Carmel, IN

The Moving Toyshop by Edmund Crispin (1946)

If you enjoy watching words at play and reading with a dictionary close at hand then Edmund Crispin is the man for you, a man who never used one word when two would do. His elaborate vocabulary and syntax, wry wit, and charmingly fey detective (Oxford don Gervase Fen) place Crispin's mysteries, along with those by Anthony Berkeley, Cyril Hare, Michael Innes and Dorothy L. Sayers, at the center of one of the richest veins in the classic British mystery mother lode.

What makes *The Moving Toyshop* the most nearly perfect of Crispin's small but sparkling output is its stunningly original and singularly silly premise. A friend of our hero Gervase Fen finds himself walking though Oxford in the wee hours; entering a deserted but unlocked toyshop on impulse, he stumbles over a dead body, which he flees to the nearest police station to report. When he leads them back to the scene of the crime, what should he find but a grocer's where just hours before the toyshop had stood, and no body in sight. The grocer, the neighbors, even the police politely insist that the vanished toyshop never existed! Who but Fen would both believe his friend's wild story and have the wiles to prove it true? As for why and how it happened — you must give yourself the pleasure of reading this delightful story to find out. Suffice it to say that Crispin follows up his clever premise with one of his liveliest plots, sending Fen and friend tearing through college, town and country after the villains with only a pocket collection of the limericks of Edward Lear to guide them.

Jill Hinckley
Murder by the Book, Portland, OR

Dreaming of the Bones by Deborah Crombie (1997)

In 1976, my husband and I lived in the village of Comberton, just outside of Cambridge, England, and down the road from Grantchester, made famous in Rupert Brooke's poetry. Richard was a visiting scholar, and I was taking time off from the graduate English program at Berkeley to do research for a paper on Virginia Woolf. We lived in the picturesquely named Dove Cottage, next door to a woman who had been at school with one of the figures in the Bloomsbury group. So it happened that in one memorable week I had tea with Frances Partridge and found a letter from Virginia Woolf carelessly stuck in a book in Dove Cottage.

These memories came vividly to life as I read Deborah Crombie's engrossing novel, *Dreaming of the Bones*. Set largely in Cambridge, Grantchester and its environs (including the village of Comberton), this is a novel that vividly captures its times and places. Victoria McClellan is a scholar writing a biography of the famous and reputedly suicidal poet of the 1960s, Lydia Brooke. Vic's work leads her to question the circumstances of Lydia's death, and when she finds manuscript pages of unpublished poems stuck in one of Lydia's books, her conviction grows that Lydia did not commit suicide. Vic calls her ex-husband, Duncan Kincaid, now a detective with Scotland Yard. He comes to Cambridge to help, assisted by his current lover and partner, Sgt. Gemma James. As Kincaid and James pursue the present day mystery, events and secrets from the past are uncovered that lead to a haunting conclusion.

In the tradition of Dorothy L. Sayers's *Gaudy Night*, which examined the life of the female academic in Oxford of the 1930s, Crombie's portrait of the woman academic and poet in Cambridge of the 1960s — and 1990s — rises above "gender analysis" without ignoring it. Most important, it's a gripping story. Fifth in her accomplished series with Kincaid and James, this novel satisfies on all levels.

Sandy Goodrick
Seattle Mystery Bookshop, Seattle, WA

The Last Good Kiss by James Crumley (1978)

Hailed after its title by *Rolling Stone* magazine as "the last good mystery," James Crumley's novel is indeed a near perfect fusion of noir style with detective form, reminiscent of only a few writers at the time, notably Charles Willeford.

The novel's first paragraph is arguably one of the great passages in mystery fiction:

When I finally caught up with Abraham Trahearne, he was drinking beer with an alcoholic bulldog named Fireball Roberts in a ramshackle joint just outside of Sonoma, California, drinking the heart right out of a fine spring afternoon.

The chase to find writer and poet Trahearne has been engineered by his ex-wife and his current wife. The chase is executed by independent, unconventional, missing-persons detective C.W. Sughrue. His primary mission accomplished, Sughrue reluctantly agrees to spend a few days looking for the Sonoma bar owner's missing daughter — a quest gleefully joined by Trahearne and Fireball.

Drinking and womanizing and pursuing leads from one dead end to another across several states, C.W. finds himself increasingly drawn to the girl he's hunting, even as his hopes for finding her dwindle away into shadows. But he too, like Fireball, is stubborn and unknowingly shortsighted about both his quarry and his companions. In time, as in all good noir fiction, it is too late to undo his actions or unspeak his words.

Crumley's prose is delicious, his powers of description — whether the landscape is interior or simply the mountains — are remarkable, and his ability to render the most delicate or difficult relationships cleanly and deeply is astonishing. Rich, meaty, and complex, *The Last Good Kiss* is inhabited by characters who are among the most memorable in all of mystery fiction but whose flaws predict their own outcomes and who lead the cunningly deceptive plot through its own fatal, flamboyant, inevitable course.

Carolyn Lane
Murder by the Book, Portland, OR

The Yellow Room Conspiracy by Peter Dickinson (1994)

The Yellow Room Conspiracy is a classic British murder mystery — a hint of the locked room problem, an English country home murder, social disgrace among the aristocracy, and a tale of coming of age in post-war Britain. It is told from the point of view of two old lovers, Paul Ackerley and Lucy Vereker, after they have been forcibly reminded of a murder each one believes the other to have committed thirty-six years earlier. Alternating chapters tell the story from either Lucy or Paul's point of view, from either the present or the past. If you can stand the slight feeling of disorientation that this causes, keep reading! Like finding your land legs, the sensation wears off and the book is well worth the perseverance.

The first Peter Dickinson novel which I remember reading was *The Old English Peep Show,* and it convinced me to keep on the lookout for any of his books. *The Yellow Room Conspiracy* is not as spectacularly original as some of Dickinson's premises (*The Glass Sided Ant's Nest* being a notable example), but has a flair for subtle detail which is hard to match.

Dickinson's style is very similar to that of Michael Innes, another sophisticated detailer of British mores in the mid-century. One of the curious points of Dickinson's style is his tendency to toss out interesting and unexpected pieces of information without making a big point of them. For example, the yellow room isn't yellow, it's green ("The Verekers were disappointed if newcomers failed to remark on its obvious greenness, thus depriving them of the chance to haul out some bound copies of *Horse and Hound* and expose the ancient saffron wallpaper behind.") The murder itself starts out straightforwardly enough, echoing Marsh's *Night at the Vulcan*, with a gas jet somehow being extinguished, but evolves into a much more complex and malign situation.

Annalisa Peterson
Kate's Mystery Books, Cambridge, MA

The Hound of the Baskervilles by Arthur Conan Doyle (1902)

Our bookstore in Tucson was originally called "Footprints of a Gigantic Hound," and mystery lovers had no doubt what the name referred to. *The Hound of the Baskervilles*, the book that resurrected Sherlock Holmes after eight years during which the great detective was presumed dead, is probably the best-known story about the world's best-known detective. Both Holmes and the hound have passed into popular culture as symbols of detection even among people who don't read mysteries.

The book is a masterful combination of eerie, supernatural atmosphere — the brooding moor, the mists, the family curse, the gigantic hellhound — and a quite satisfactorily rational explanation at the end. Like all the Holmes stories, one of its most enjoyable features is the interplay of character, usually centered on Watson's awe at Holmes' amazing ability to form correct hypotheses from observing apparently insignificant details.

Arthur Conan Doyle's creation has inspired numerous imitators. The cerebral detective and the amiable sidekick appear again and again in various forms (Poirot and Hastings, Wolfe and Goodwin, for instance), and Holmes pastiches are so numerous they almost form a separate subgenre. Returning to Doyle himself after reading the disciples, however, I am always struck by the skill of the master. The supple prose, the believable dialogue, the touches of irony (especially about Holmes' competitiveness and vanity), the ability to create atmosphere and character with a few quick strokes — all these explain why these books still draw us when countless others have become dated and lifeless. Both for its precedent-setting influence over other mystery writers, and as a masterpiece in its own right, *The*

Hound ranks at the top of our 100 list.

Patricia Davis
Clues Unlimited, Tucson, AZ

Rebecca by Daphne du Maurier (1938)

Last night I dreamt I went to Manderley again.

Surely, there are few opening lines better known than this. I first read this book many years ago and thought I had forgotten much of it, but that one sentence opened the closet door to my memory.

Rebecca is not a typical mystery. Romance is a large part of the story and all the elements of a gothic novel are here — beautiful young wife, brooding older husband, mean-spirited housekeeper and Manderley itself, a house of secrets, looming at the edge of a stormy sea. What sets this apart from other gothic fiction is Daphne du Maurier's superb gift as a story-teller. Even the heroine, who is annoyingly insecure in today's atmosphere of strong-willed women, is a sympathetic character in the author's way of telling the tale.

The puzzle is solved three-quarters of the way into the book and, for me, the real strength of the author's work lies in what happens after the solution and what I learn about the causes and consequences of the original crime. Are there times when murder might be justified or, at least, understood if not condoned? When is it appropriate for others to choose their own interpretations of bare facts?

These questions, and more, are what made *Rebecca* so fascinating to me all those years ago and they still do today. Perhaps the greatest mystery of all — and one I'll probably never solve — is why does our heroine have no name? I have to assume the author had a reason for this omission. How I would love to be able to ask her!

Lelia T. Taylor
Creatures 'n Crooks Bookshoppe, Richmond, VA

Booked to Die by John Dunning (1992)

Readers carry around mental lists of the books important in their lives. Occasionally such a list will include one book that was literally life-changing. For me that book was John Dunning's *Booked to Die*; the book introduced a new generation to book collecting just as Christopher Morley's *The Haunted Bookshop* did an earlier generation.

Cliff Janeway is the book's complex hero — a tough homicide detective fed up with the justice system and a reader with a passion for book collecting. As Janeway investigates the murder of book scout Bobby Westfall, he leads us through the Denver book world of Colfax Avenue — "Bookman's Row." Throughout the murder investigation, Janeway is compelled to examine his own career in law enforcement and his feelings about the criminal justice system. When he quits the police force to become a book dealer himself, he recognizes that "for the first time in years, I knew where I was going." But with another deft twist, two more murders on Bookman's Row force Janeway back into his old life as a detective — this time without the shield of the Denver PD.

A terrific mystery? Definitely! A memorable book? Oh yes. A book that speaks to the heart and is truly life changing? Well, it certainly was for me. You see, in 1996 I read *Booked To Die* and *The Bookman's Wake,* the second Janeway mystery. In 1998, I was fortunate enough to meet John Dunning in Denver — the day before I enrolled in the Antiquarian Book School in Colorado Springs. And today as I sit in the sawdust of my very own, soon-to-be open mystery bookstore, I remember what Janeway said when he opened Twice Told Books:

I walked through the store and only then did it hit me — what I had taken on, what I'd left behind, how drastically my life had changed in only one month. The place smelled of paint fumes and sawdust. It was real, it was alive, and it was mine. I had a sense of proprietorship, of direction.

Jane Hooper
Sherlock's Home, Liberty, MO

41

Old Bones by Aaron Elkins (1987)

Old Bones is the fourth in the Gideon Oliver series by Aaron Elkins. This book won the Edgar Award and certainly deserved it. Gideon Oliver is an anthropology professor in Port Angeles, Washington. He is also a modern-day Sherlock Holmes. From a few bones he can tell many things about the person to whom they belonged. And when he explains it to the layman, it becomes very logical. I also enjoy the relationship between Oliver and his wife. They are both very likable characters.

In *Old Bones*, Oliver is a guest speaker at the Eighth Annual Conference on Science and Detection in St. Malo when he is invited by Police Inspector Lucien Joly to inspect a skeleton discovered by workers digging in a cellar to repair some pipes. This seems to be the perfect case for Oliver, who is also known as the "Skeleton Detective." He uncovers a crime that was committed over forty years earlier, during World War II, and that might be connected to the recent death of the owner of the house. Gideon Oliver, with the assistance of John Lau, an FBI man from Hawaii, uncovers a love affair hidden for years which provides clues to the two murders.

Elkins also won an award for his series about Chris Norgren, an art museum curator in Seattle, Washington. And with his wife, Charlotte, he writes a golf mystery series featuring golfer Lee Ofsted and her policeman boyfriend, Graham Sheldon.

As I read the Gideon Oliver series, I feel the enjoyment of having discovered a successor to my old favorite, Sherlock Holmes. These are some of the few books that I reread simply for a good story.

Patsy Asher
Remember the Alibi Mystery Bookstore, San Antonio, TX

One for the Money by Janet Evanovich (1994)

Janet Evanovich and Stephanie Plum hit the mystery world in 1994, taking no prisoners, but providing a lot of entertainment for their readers.

One for the Money is the start of a fresh, innovative series and introduces Stephanie Plum, who lives in Trenton, New Jersey (aka the "burg") and is looking for work. She had been a lingerie buyer, and as we meet her, she joins her cousin's bail bond agency as a "bounty hunter" with little experience but a lot of sass. There is a great sense of place, a feeling you have actually been to Jersey.

Intriguing characters abound in the series, few more engaging than Granny Mazur. When I picture Granny in my mind, I see Estelle Getty in *The Golden Girls,* but with a gun. As the series progresses, characters are added to the considerable delight of this reader. Nor are there just interesting humans. Stephanie also has a hamster named Rex, and later in the series acquires my favorite dog, a golden retriever.

There is never a dull moment with Stephanie Plum, whether she is having problems with recalcitrant bail jumpers, family complications, or her increasing vehicle demolition tally. Yes, our Stephanie goes through vehicles the way some people go through chocolate chip cookies.

She also has a romantic entanglement with her first love, now a Jersey cop, Morelli, a true hunk with an attitude. As the series continued, I got very interested in what might happen to the "relationship" between Stephanie and Morelli.

One for the Money is an entertaining and refreshing look at the world of bounty hunting and life in New Jersey with all its joys and traumas. I enjoy the series and always hate to finish one book because I know the wait for the next one will be too long. I frequently am caught laughing out loud when reading the series. I would love to hang with Stephanie and friends, but I would never loan her my car!

Maggie Mason
Lookin for Books, San Diego, CA

Time and Again by Jack Finney (1970)

The Gilded Age has never been more gilded than in my imagination. Perhaps it is because I grew up hearing tales about my great-grandmother who kept house for her brother, the proverbial Irish saloon-keeper, in the late 1880s, and stories about my grandmother, a milliner on the Magnificent Mile in the early 1900s. Whatever it is, the era from the Franco-Prussian War of 1870 to the Edwardian age is mesmerizing to me. The mystery that captures that long-ago era most profoundly for me is Jack Finney's *Time and Again*.

This unique book glides gracefully across time, as well as several different genres. Not only is it a masterpiece of time travel, it is a cunningly wicked mystery. The premise is deceptively simple: the mysterious Ruben Prien, acting on behalf of the US government, is recruiting suitable candidates to study the possibility of Einstein's theory of time. Simon Morley, a young advertising illustrator in New York, proves himself to be admirably qualified, and even suggests a plausible reason to journey to New York, 1882: he wants to see a letter being mailed. This letter, which is in the possession of Si's woman friend Kate Mancuso, has caused much heartbreak in the family that adopted her. At first Si is only sent to observe, but as Si returns again and again to the world of the Tweed Ring and all the political ferment of the late nineteenth century, he inevitably becomes more involved in the actual events of that tumultuous time.

The care with which Finney constructed this amazing book is evident on every page. The costumes, characters, and customs of old New York are depicted with loving detail, underpinned by the mysterious letter. Finney's themes of government greed, the responsibility of the individual for the consequences of an action, the conflict between science and ethics, are all the more striking for their contemporaneity. The climax is chilling in its final plot twist, and in the brilliance of Simon's resolute but subtle action.

Finney's novel shines with a magic that time cannot dim. It

reminds me why fiction sometimes holds more truth than science does: Einstein gave us a theory, but Finney gives us the reason for the journey.

Gilly Parker
Kate's Mystery Books, Cambridge, MA

Who in Hell Is Wanda Fuca? by G.M. Ford (1995)

Seattle Mystery Bookshop has a good customer who used to come in and say, "I could write books better than a lot you have here," and we'd say "Yeah, sure, Jerry." Then one day he came in and said "My mystery's going to be published," and we said (to ourselves), "Uh oh, what'll we do if it's awful?" But when we eventually read the manuscript of *Who in Hell Is Wanda Fuca?* we knew our worries were over.

In his first recorded case, Seattle private eye Leo Waterman engages the help of "the boys," a ragtag group of down-and-outs who make excellent field observers. "The destitute and homeless had become so prevalent and so bothersome in Seattle that they were able to operate under a cloak of cultural invisibility. They were there, but nobody saw them." The book's title, with its terrible but memorable geographic pun, comes from a remark by one of the boys in a well-oiled moment; the only straits Leo gets into are desperate but figurative. With its emphasis on environmentalism and social issues, and its acerbically humorous voice, *Wanda* is a sparkling example of 1990s Pacific Northwest noir. And the promise that's shown in this first novel continues in subsequent books with Leo and the boys.

Gerald Manson Ford was right: he *can* write books better than a lot of the others we have in our store.

Bill Farley
Seattle Mystery Bookshop, Seattle, WA

Whip Hand by Dick Francis (1979)

Grand Master Dick Francis writes what he knows. A former steeplechase jockey, he retired from racing at age 36, and six years later published his first mystery novel. Since 1962 he's been writing a book a year.

Whatever aspect of the equine world is involved, his love of the creatures is apparent. These are not "horse books," however, but terrific mysteries that manage to be stories of courage, determination and adversity overcome. Francis speaks to the flaws in us all, and makes his protagonists real, human characters that we genuinely like. Along the way, he gives us a believable and consistently well-plotted page turner. His research is masterful, and he deftly ensures that we "get it" in such a way as to feel somewhat pleased with ourselves. (To my mind, the ability to do that regularly with such seeming effortlessness is a pretty good trick in itself.)

With a couple of exceptions, his novels are stand-alones. Jockey Sid Halley has been in three: *Odds Against, Whip Hand* and *Come to Grief.*

In *Odds Against*, Sid is in a bad way. His marriage is over, and he's been forced to retire from racing due to a fall that crushed both his left hand and his spirit. He accepts a consultant's position to an investigative firm that specializes in racing and gradually comes back to life.

Whip Hand, the 1979 Edgar and Gold Dagger winner, is a zinger! Sid now has his own agency and is working two cases: a painful one, wherein he has to clear his ex-wife's (hence, his own) name, and a mystery thrust on him by a former employer. Do the losses of their most promising horses constitute a conspiracy or just hysterical imaginings? This book explores Sid's darkest terrors, splintering and reintegrating his character once again. It provides a fascinating look into both veterinary medicine and human greed. Absolutely ingenious plot and a breathtaking conclusion.

Mary Ann McDonald
Capital Crimes Mystery Bookstore, Sacramento, CA

The Hours Before Dawn by Celia Fremlin (1958)

I'd give anything — anything — for a night's sleep.

Anyone who's ever had a baby in the household will acknowledge the validity of the first sentence of this Edgar winning novel. Like most classic English mysteries, *The Hours Before Dawn* is a comedy of manners, a masterpiece of social observation etched in black humor that follows the relations between Louise Henderson, a middle-class housewife, and her nosy neighbors, demanding friends, insensitive husband, condescending mother-in-law and ill-behaved children. Into this mess steps the strangely familiar Miss Vera Brandon, the new boarder, a woman "of a certain age," who is both a classics scholar and immensely strong.

But *The Hours Before Dawn* is also a great suspense novel, the vividly written evocation of a mind at work under extreme stress. Celia Fremlin wanted to express a major human experience, living with a newborn, that had never been treated seriously before, and she succeeded, as Louise's sleep-deprived reveries enter a sinister dreamscape whose menacing specters become terrifyingly real.

Nonseries crime fiction by women is often unjustly neglected, dismissed as the "had-I-but-known" school. Even some readers who favor women protagonists might find the heroine of this book wimpy because she acts more like a real woman than a fantasy figure like Kinsey Millhone. But what Fremlin is really showing is the powerlessness of many woman in '50s society, and how resourceful they had to be in order to survive. Those who underestimate "simple" wives and mothers like Louise Henderson should remember the fate of the independent superwoman Miss Brandon. As Louise's mother-in-law says, what some people call a doormat is, in fact, the toughest mat in the house.

Jamie Agnew
Aunt Agatha's, Ann Arbor, MI

A Great Deliverance by Elizabeth George (1988)

Like many great first novels, *A Great Deliverance* is so seamless, so beautifully written and executed, that it's hard to believe it *is* a first novel. Embroidering and deepening a classic genre, the English detective story, George has made the form her own with the depth of character development and psychological motive she brings to her crime puzzles. She has used the mystery series form to develop characterization to a practically unheard of depth. Inspector Thomas Lynley's heritage is definitely by way of Ngaio Marsh's Roderick Alleyn (professional, yet titled), and he is even more a modern echo of Dorothy L. Sayers' classic creation, Lord Peter Wimsey. He is more unsure of himself than Wimsey, more constrained by actually working within the police force, and George's mind is not so taken up with devilishly clever clues as in laying the groundwork for psychological horror.

The murder that Lynley is trying to resolve in *A Great Deliverance* is a gruesome one: a man has been found with his head cut off in his farmyard, his dead dog lying at his side, his daughter sitting calmly near the body with an ax in her hand. The daughter has been put into a mental institution by her cousin. Lynley is sure there is more to the case. What makes a George novel so compulsively readable is finding out the *why* of the crime. Since the plot is determined by the characters, the ending is at the same time a shocking surprise, and a necessary resolution.

I think George's real genius may be in describing, succinctly and all too memorably, the private hell of the many different characters the reader encounters in her novels. In a brisk paragraph, she can lay in the awful parameters of someone's life and that someone may stay with you long after you have put down the book. Her other stroke of genius is that she has taken two very different core characters, Lynley and Detective Sergeant Barbara Havers, and nearly dared them to be able to tolerate each other and work together. This is far from one novel's journey, but it's certainly finely established in *A Great Deliverance.*

Robin Agnew
Aunt Agatha's, Ann Arbor, MI

Smallbone Deceased by Michael Gilbert (1950)

Smallbone Deceased is a splendid example of witty detective fiction at its best. Gilbert, himself a solicitor, writes about a firm of solicitors so old-fashioned and stodgy that the senior partner has listed proper closings for letters written by junior members of the organization to dukes, countesses and other aristocrats who make up much of their clientele. An irreverent younger lawyer tells a new colleague that their reference books are Burke and Debrett, and that they are probably "the last firm in London that draws up strict marriage settlements and calls the heir up on his twenty-first birthday to execute a disentailing deed and drink a glass of pre-1914 sherry."

The story opens at a staff dinner at which Abel Horniman, the founder and senior partner, is eulogized by his partners. Soon after, one of Horniman's least favorite clients, and a cotrustee of the Ichabod Stokes Trust, is found dead in a large deed box in Horniman's office. The diminutive corpse of Marcus Smallbone fills the space that should be taken by documents relating to the trust. A delightful cast of characters, an array of suspects, an ingenious plot and a suspenseful conclusion make this a memorable tale. Gilbert's satirical portrait of the legal profession must have inspired Sarah Caudwell, the star of the next generation of comic legal mystery writers.

Some American mystery readers met Michael Gilbert at the London Bouchercon (1990), and enjoyed hearing him talk about this work. He, Caudwell and Michael Underwood were on a panel about legal mysteries. When asked their favorite writer of legal mysteries, they all agreed their favorite was Cyril Hare, a slightly earlier practitioner of the art. Gilbert's mysteries fit into the tradition of the best English thrillers, and *Smallbone Deceased* is an outstanding example.

Mary Helen Becker
Booked for Murder, Madison, WI

"A" Is For Alibi by Sue Grafton (1982)

By now, everyone knows that Sue Grafton wrote *"A" Is for Alibi* as a legal way to kill her ex-husband during a messy divorce. From that ingenious motive, the mystery world was changed forever as her sleuth, Kinsey Millhone, joined other newly created female PIs, Marcia Muller's Sharon McCone and Sara Paretsky's V.I. Warshawski, in the hardcore world previously inhabited exclusively by men. In this first of the alphabet mysteries, Kinsey is hired by the second wife of divorce lawyer Laurence Fife, who was murdered more than eight years before. Her new client has just finished serving a prison term for his murder. Now she wants Kinsey to identify the real killer. During Kinsey's investigation of the family and business life of the victim, no one escapes her sleuthing, even her client. Her unraveling of the past leading up to the murder is a classic example of the onion-peeling technique employed in the traditional PI novel.

Kinsey lives in "Santa Teresa," a fictionalized southern California town invented by Ross Macdonald, genius creator of Lew Archer, which bears strong similarities to Santa Barbara, the home of both authors. In contrast to the males of the genre at that time, Kinsey freely expresses compassion for the victims of the unspeakable (and illegal) personal and professional abuses that are scattered throughout this wealthy town. Gifted with a razor-sharp sense of humor and strong sense of self, Kinsey immediately embedded herself in the hearts and minds of readers.

Judy Duhl
Scotland Yard Books, Winnetka, IL

The Killings at Badger's Drift by Caroline Graham (1987)

What did retired teacher Miss Emily Simpson see in the woods that so upset her that she ran home? What so distracted her that she neglected to tell her best friend Lucy Bellringer about the spurred coral root orchid she'd just found? What did she see that so threatened someone that she was murdered before morning? In order to solve Miss Simpson's murder, Detective Chief Inspector Barnaby, assisted by the frequently peeved Sergeant Troy, must unravel many more of the mysteries of the village of Badger's Drift where nearly everyone has reason to lie: the pompous village doctor, his frightened sexy wife, and his lumpy teenage daughter; the village "squire" and his frustrated sister; his lovely fiancée and her strange artist brother; and a brutish property manager.

Caroline Graham's debut is a stunning example of the quintessentially English cozy-with-procedural-overtones. It features all the characteristics of the traditional English mystery that Agatha Christie created for her sleuth Miss Marple, but instead of the amateur asking questions and pursuing leads, the local investigative team consists of professionals who use the influence of their offices to corner the culprit. Unlike the more modern and largely American police procedural, however, Graham's novels — like Ruth Rendell's (the Kingsmarkham novels), Peter Robinson's and Jill McGown's — use modern scientific investigative techniques sparingly and/or inconclusively. The solutions are largely dependent on the analysis of the detective protagonist, whose life and family feature prominently throughout the series.

Kathy Phillips
Spenser's Mystery Bookshop, Boston, MA

The Man With a Load of Mischief by Martha Grimes (1981)

The English inn stands permanently planted at the confluence of the roads of history, memory, and romance.

So wrote Martha Grimes in her fine first novel, *The Man with a Load of Mischief*, which is named, like all her subsequent Richard Jury novels, after an English pub. For Grimes, the pub is the starting point, giving her mysteries an instantly rich setting, tying them to the great Golden Age of the past, while at the same time bringing her own gifts of vigorous, lively prose to the task of telling a good story. She draws wittily and cogently on many of the elements brought to life in the Golden Age — locked room puzzles, a dignified Scotland Yard Inspector, and a cast of characters as well rounded and diverse as any reader could ever ask for.

In using the handsome, clever Melrose Plant as a sort of sidekick to Inspector Jury, she also draws together an amateur and a professional detective, who in this and many other Grimes novels, draw on their separate and not inconsiderable skills to help each other solve more than one case. I'm not sure which of these two men is the more dishy — the wealthy Plant, snobbishly rejecting his title but enjoying his luxuries, or the hard working, melancholy, sensitive Richard Jury. One thing I do suspect: Grimes hasn't paired either of them off romantically because she'd like to keep them for herself. And who can blame her? In Plant and Jury she has created two of the most appealing male characters in modern detective fiction.

In *The Man With a Load of Mischief*, Grimes has crafted a clever locked room puzzle with a body count high enough to rival Agatha Christie's, as well as a secret from the past hinted at throughout the novel but only finally fleshed out in the last few riveting chapters. Chief Inspector Jury uses his wits and little else to escape the clutches of a criminal, and the aftermath of the crime, in typical Golden Age fashion, leaves most characters better off. What may set Martha Grimes apart above all else is the confidence and real joy she has in telling her stories — for that alone they deserve to be read for many, many years.

Robin Agnew
Aunt Agatha's, Ann Arbor, MI

The Maltese Falcon by Dashiell Hammett (1930)

The Maltese Falcon first appeared 70 years ago, and it has not been dulled at all by age — it's every bit as shocking now as when it was released. It begins with two private eyes, Sam Spade and Miles Archer, interviewing a client, a good-looking redheaded dame. Archer is obviously a brute, while Spade comes off as smoother and yet devilish — the more likable of the two, but not to say any nicer. The redhead employs Archer to tail a man that evening, and when she leaves, the two detectives banter about their real reasons for taking the job (her looks and her money). No knights in shining armor, these two.

That night, Archer is led up a blind alley and killed. Upon notification, Spade doesn't even pretend he cares. Soon a couple of thick-necked cops arrive at his apartment to accuse Spade of gunning down the man Archer was tailing, who has also turned up dead. Meanwhile, Spade's secretary thinks Spade killed Archer himself; after all, Spade has been sleeping with Archer's wife. And when Spade finally finds his client, she tells him a completely different story than she did the day before. He's bothered by her duplicity — but not so much that he objects to her seducing him.

It would be unfair to reveal any more of the plot, but things only get thicker, and no true hero ever appears. Dashiell Hammett's unflinching narrative eye enables him to depict a world populated exclusively by selfish, greedy people with no desire to defend their actions, and the overall atmosphere is one of almost inhuman cold. If anything, it is this harshness that makes *The Maltese Falcon* such a classic — this is vintage noir, and the darkness here is not in the atmosphere but the very soul of the novel.

Andrew Necci
Creatures 'n Crooks Bookshoppe, Richmond, VA

An English Murder by Cyril Hare (1951)
(aka The Christmas Murder)

Cyril Hare, pseudonym for lawyer and judge Alfred Alexander Gordon Clark (1900-1958), was perhaps better known in Canada and in the UK than he was in the US. Although his output was small, he remains an important contributor to the world of detective fiction. His two principal characters were Francis Pettigrew, a small-time lawyer, and Inspector Mallett, a Scotland Yard detective. *An English Murder* is arguably his most important and enjoyable contribution to the field, and it features neither of these characters. This is one of those perfect novels that can be enjoyed more than once and can be so easily recommended to all fans of the Christie school. It is short enough to have few wasted words (unlike so many recent offerings, bloated to the point of bursting, over-word-processed and under-edited) and long enough to give you all the plot and character development that you can reasonably use. Those curmudgeons Barzun and Taylor in the revised *A Catalogue of Crime,* found it to be "unduly short and not very substantial" but they hedge by saying "perhaps."

This is a Christmas mystery, that time of the year which is supposed to be of peace and joy, of good cheer and good will, but, if detective novels are enough of a reflection of real life, which turns out so often to be a time of mayhem and malice. *An English Murder* is a wonderful example of a Christmas mystery. It also has elements of the locked room mystery: a Christmas party in a rundown castle, locked in by snow and overflowing streams; a small cast of characters including an impoverished peer, the faithful butler and an ambitious daughter. With wit and style the author produces an English murder that is a delight. The only thing wrong with the book? It's out of print and has been for most of the 1990s.

J.D. Singh
Sleuth of Baker Street, Toronto, Canada

The Silence of the Lambs by Thomas Harris (1988)

Only one serial killer novel is superior to *The Silence of the Lambs*, and that is *Red Dragon*, the book in which Thomas Harris introduces Hannibal Lecter, arguably crime fiction's most terrifying villain.

Clarice Starling, an ambitious young FBI trainee, becomes involved in a case of the serial killer who is known as "Buffalo Bill" because he humps his victims and skins them.

In exchange for small favors, the jailed Dr. Lecter offers to help Starling. She is empowered to have him moved to a more comfortable prison with a week each year during which he will be allowed outside on a guarded island.

The power-hungry head of the new facility visits Lecter and he makes his own deal with the brilliant psychopath. All the information Hannibal (The Cannibal) imparts is phony and he quickly escapes from the new facility.

As the rest of the FBI team goes off on its wild goose chase as orchestrated by Lecter, Starling tracks down Buffalo Bill and has a final confrontation with him as she tries to save his most recently imprisoned victim.

Although this is a terribly violent and graphic novel, Harris' extraordinary skill positively compels the reader to continue turning pages, even while revulsed by certain scenes. Unhappily, the staggering success of the book lured other, less talented, writers into the serial killer genre, writers whose idea of creativity is to depict more and more gruesome acts of unspeakable violence while paying little heed to the notions of character development and plot, both of which Harris accomplished in an exemplary fashion.

The Silence of the Lambs was made into a wonderful film in 1991, providing Jodie Foster with her finest screen role and Anthony Hopkins with an Academy Award for his memorable portrayal of evil incarnate.

Otto Penzler
The Mysterious Bookshop, New York, NY

Tourist Season by Carl Hiaasen (1986)

Violent yet extremely humorous, momentarily entertaining yet long-term thought-provoking, dark yet airy and light. These contradictions just barely begin to describe *Tourist Season*. It's a must read for anyone whose idea of a great book is one that evokes the whole range of emotions while keeping the reader frantically turning the pages.

The story begins in sunny Miami, where trouble is brewing, in the form of a series of murders and disappearances of tourists and Floridians involved with the tourist trade. Brian Keyes, reporter turned private investigator, jumps into the fray, hoping to solve the mystery of who is responsible for the crimes. He finds himself in great personal danger, which intensifies as the story continues.

Along with Brian, there is a fascinatingly drawn cast of characters, some heroic and some evil. The setting, too, is well described, and Carl Hiaasen brings the people and places to life.

What's more, there's real humor in this story. Hiaasen excels in evoking laughter at some very unexpected events. By this laughter, we are reminded that, after all, this is fiction, but it is fiction with a real message. What makes this book unique and eminently deserving of inclusion in this list is the way in which it mixes mystery and message. Yes, it's a real puzzler! The need to know, first, who are the perpetrators, and second, how will they be stopped, keeps the reader avidly and actively involved.

The staying power of Hiaasen's book lies in the theme that a wistful wish to turn back the clock can, in the wrong hands, lead to disaster. Then there's the belief, held by more than a few people, that the rightness of their goal gives them the authority to take any action to achieve it. Hiaasen explores and explodes these ideas, leavening his presentation with humor and suspense, making *Tourist Season* a winner in any season.

Stephanie Saxon Levine
Murder on Miami Beach, North Miami Beach, FL

The Talented Mr. Ripley by Patricia Highsmith (1955)

"Much more sinister and disturbing than the recent film version" is one way I describe *The Talented Mr. Ripley* to customers. Tom Ripley is the main character (but never the hero) of Patricia Highsmith's classic thriller set in the 1950s.

As the story opens, Tom is concerned that he is being followed by the police, and that he will soon hear "Tom Ripley, you are under arrest!" Right from the first page, Highsmith makes the reader wonder about Ripley, wonder why he would be expecting the police, wonder why he readily agrees to go to Europe to look for the errant son of a wealthy man, and wonder who Tom Ripley really is.

The search for Dickie Greenleaf takes Tom to Mongibello, Italy. After meeting him, Tom begins to weave his way into Dickie's life, becoming obsessed with Dickie's charming manner and unlimited access to money; Dickie seems equally charmed by Tom's attentions. By the time Tom's money begins to run out and his fascination with Dickie begins to fade, the reader is not surprised by the solution that he arrives at. Murder, followed by impersonation, seems logical to Ripley and his methods, which combine luck and careful planning, are chilling.

The strength of the story lies in the balance created between the insights Highsmith provides into Ripley's character, and those which readers must create for themselves. Tom Ripley is still a mystery to me: I wonder about him, about his childhood, his obsession with belonging, the fact that "he was himself and yet not himself. He felt blameless and free..." As I remind people, Ripley is not the hero of this story or of any of the four subsequent novels in which he is featured. He is, however, unforgettable.

Jean May
Murder by the Book, Portland, OR

On Beulah Height by Reginald Hill (1998)

There is simply no other character in contemporary crime fiction quite like Andy Dalziel, or "the fat bastard" as friends and enemies alike often refer to him. Coarse, capricious, unsentimental (at least on the surface), and unfailingly un-politically correct, Dalziel is one of those characters whom readers will either come to love or just can't tolerate. Teamed with the long-suffering and much less colorful Peter Pascoe, Dalziel faces the most haunting case of his career in Hill's masterpiece, *On Beulah Height.*

Years before, young Dalziel was on the case when three little girls disappeared in the village of Dendale. The crimes were never solved; no perpetrator was ever brought to justice. Then the town was abandoned and flooded to make a reservoir. Twelve years later, however, a drought has slowly brought the ghostly village of Dendale back into view, and with it, the memories of those unsolved crimes. Another child has gone missing from a nearby village: Dalziel feels that this case must be connected with those earlier, unsolved ones and he's deter-mined to find the answers. Hill creates some of the most intricate plots, memorable characters and richly detailed back-grounds in crime fiction, and *On Beulah Height* shows him at the summit of his considerable powers.

Other standouts among his oeuvre are *A Pinch of Snuff, Deadheads, Pictures of Perfection* and *The Wood Beyond.* He is truly one of the finest writers of crime fiction in the twentieth century and has been awarded the Cartier Diamond Dagger for Lifetime Achievement from the Crime Writers Association in the United Kingdom.

Dean James
Murder by the Book, Houston, TX

A Thief of Time by Tony Hillerman (1988)

Almost any book Tony Hillerman writes would rate high on

my list of all time favorites. Why? Mostly because of all the Indian stuff. Tony tells the story about selling his first book and an agent (I think it was an agent) told him to get rid of all the Indian stuff. Tony didn't do that — but he found an editor who liked reading about the southwest and the Navajo, and the rest is history.

A Thief of Time satisfies on many levels. Lieutenant Joe Leaphorn is depressed because his beloved Emma died and he's even resigned from the police. You feel Leaphorn's pain in dealing with his grief and yet you know — all he really needs is a new mystery to solve. He does becomes intrigued, despite himself, in the mysterious disappearance of a woman anthropologist. His path crosses with young officer Jim Chee. Chee finds a couple of dead men at an ancient burial ground. Chee is still somewhat in awe of Leaphorn and Leaphorn still has doubts that Chee will ever amount to anything. The relationship of the two as their investigations keep crisscrossing gives us such insights and deepens their characters and you have the sense that one day they might even be friends.

The Indian lore and legends give you a strong sense of place and a small understanding of the people. You feel the desert heat, the vastness of the empty harsh lands and yet see the beauty in that same land. We've visited parts of the Arizona and New Mexico reservation lands and the colorful canyons and deserts somehow make up for the bleakness and isolation.

The title, *A Thief of Time*, refers to the vandals who steal or destroy the ancient artifacts and steal from the historical time lines. Hillerman gives you background and histories of these artifacts, so that you also gain knowledge as you read.

As the book draws to a close, Leaphorn's relationship with Chee is strengthened and best of all, Leaphorn feels like living again. There is mystery and magic in Hillerman's work and we can only hope Leaphorn and Chee are around to thrill us for many moons.

Jan Grape
Mysteries & More Online, Austin, TX

Cotton Comes to Harlem by Chester Himes (1965)

Chester Himes has been both lauded as a writer of great literature and slammed as a sellout to Hollywood. *Cotton Comes to Harlem* can be read today as a fairly accurate take upon ghetto life in a large northern city neighborhood at the time. *Cotton* brought back too many memories for me of growing up in just such an environment at just that same time. Himes must be a very skilled writer if a so-called "minor" work can elicit such strong reactions. I didn't really want to be reminded of the dirt, the jive, the scams, the booze, the dope, the ugliness and cruelties that often prevailed, but his writing also brought back the kindnesses, the trust and caring of loved ones, and the belief that all could come right in the end, somehow.

Cotton also has a wickedly subtle and sly sense of humor. The novel opens with a scene of a revivalist-type preacher holding a rally to sell passage on ships back to Africa for "just" $1000 per family. That's a heck of a lot of money in 1965 dollars especially in this neighborhood, and yet 87 families have already signed on the dotted line. Not surprisingly, someone else finds the idea of so much money conveniently gathered in a central location to be very appealing as well, and another set of thieves shows up.

The writing style is similar to '40s noir, with edges softened a bit and with current 1960s references. The good guys are a couple of hard-nosed, hard-edged cops who've put their lives on the line often, and don't handle failure very well. The interaction between Coffin Ed and Grave Digger seems genuinely caring, and they are entertaining characters. Their sense of humor is edgy and sly, and I liked them very much despite their penchant for large weapons; they are brought to life with a sense of loving kindness by the author.

Himes finds many ways of eliciting anger and unhappiness, showing kindness or cruelty, giving hope or showcasing despair. *Cotton Comes to Harlem* is a funny and involved mystery, well-written and complex, with as many layers as you want to pull back at any given time.

AbiGail Hamilton
Black Bird Mysteries, Keedysville, MD

Hamlet, Revenge by Michael Innes (1937)

... he now pushed Appleby into the lift and cried "Down!" so fiercely that the already overwrought lift-boy lost his head and shot them straight to the top floor. It was, Appleby thought, an excellent prelude to adventure.

As a big fan of Shakespeare, I was thrilled to find another author had taken the pains to create a mystery involving the bard's work. The story is set in the 1930s in England at a weekend party where the distinguished guests are putting on *Hamlet*. During the production, one of the actors is shot and killed. The suspects are Hamlet, the Queen, Rosencrantz, Guildenstern and all of the other cast members including the ghost and the prompter. A catchy thing about Michael Innes is his style of metaphors. He has a way of explaining situations that gives a thrill to the mind. He has the classic English cottage mystery with all of the familiar players; the country bobbies, the thoughtful detective, the upper-class household where all of the servants must be interrogated. With his Agatha Christie feel, Innes has brought us another classic world to love. If I could write like anybody, I would want to write like Innes. He has created characters to admire and hate, with depth and mystery in each person.

Ann Saunders
Murder, Mystery & Mayhem, Farmington, MI

An Unsuitable Job for a Woman by P.D. James (1972)

Not only is P.D. James a touchstone for my generation of women — one of the first women to combine elegant prose with the nuances of psychological mysteries and the sometimes grisly details of homicide and police work — but she provided us with another touchstone in the character of Cordelia Gray, a private investigator. This is vintage James; vintage in the best sense of the word. Like fine wine, this book has aged well. In some ways so timely, it is startling to recall it was published almost 30 years ago. Endued with wonderful descriptive writing, from sketches distilling the essence of a character into a pithy phrase to a description of a painting so vivid it seems you are gazing at it in a museum, this novel is impressive for its prose alone. But James never forgets that she is first and foremost a mystery writer, and delightful as these descriptions are, they only enhance the procedure as Cordelia perseveres in her investigation.

The opening is gripping, and sets up the ultimate irony. Cordelia discovers her erstwhile partner has committed suicide; she is then hired on her first case alone to investigate another suicide, that of a man younger than she is. Sir Ronald Callender, a prominent scientist, wants to know the circumstances of his son Mark's suicide. This young man had left a promising career at Cambridge University just before the end of the term, and had hired himself out as a gardener. Since Mark was largely ignored by his prominent father, Cordelia gains little knowledge of the young man in his strange household. She must find her clues for his uncharacteristic behavior from his friends at Cambridge and from his mother's old nanny, dismissed from service shortly after his mother's death. In her meticulous and patient retracing of the last few weeks of Mark's life, Cordelia proves herself every bit as professional as that mythical and irritating (to her) figure of Adam Dalgliesh.

In the wake of V.I., Kinsey and Sharon, we sometimes tend to forget that first there was Cordelia, standing alone bravely if a little uncertainly, thoughtfully pursuing her unsuitable job. There is such a direct line between *A Room of One's Own* and *An Unsuitable Job for a Woman*, it makes one a bit sad that Virginia Woolf didn't live to read this fine mystery. She would have been proud.

Gilly Parker
Kate's Mystery Books, Cambridge, MA

The Ritual Bath by Faye Kellerman (1986)

The Ritual Bath is the first in a surprising series that combines excellent mystery, interesting characters and a glance into Jewish rituals and traditions. In the California hills outside of Los Angeles a small yeshiva has been having some problems with the neighboring community. Their world is turned upside down when one of the women leaving the mikva, the ritual bath, is attacked. Peter Decker of the LAPD arrives and finds that no one at the yeshiva is willing to cooperate except Rina Decker, a teacher and the caretaker of the mikva.

As Peter tries to work the case, he is thwarted at almost every turn due to religious law. Rina tries to help him and the more she helps, the more he becomes interested in her. Peter begins to worry that perhaps Rina is the next intended victim of a crime even worse than the prior woman's rape.

When I first read this book I thought it was well written, and I loved it even more when I reread it. I learned even more the second time I read this book. My favorite kind of mystery combines a good story and also allows the reader to learn something. This book definitely qualifies. As a Jewish woman, I feel this is a wonderful way for people to learn about Judaism, its laws and its rituals. It is one of the books I recommend.

Paige Rose
Mystery Loves Company, Baltimore, MD

When the Bough Breaks by Jonathan Kellerman (1985) (aka Shrunken Heads)

I discovered Jonathan Kellerman's books while I was taking a college class called Psychopathology. No offense to the professor or the textbook, but Jonathan Kellerman's psychologist, Alex Delaware, was a far more interesting read.

Alex Delaware is a burnt out child psychologist. At 33, he is already retired. His final group of patients consisted of children who were molested by their day-care's owner's husband, a heartbreaking situation which concluded with Alex finding the molester dead in his office.

Six months later and Alex is still trying to cope. One morning, Milo Sturgis, cop and friend, shows up at Alex's door. He needs help. A child is the only possible witness to the death of a psychologist and his girlfriend. The little girl, Melody, cannot seem to remember what she saw. Milo is hoping Alex can hypnotize her into remembering. This push is all that Alex needs. With newfound purpose, Alex throws himself into helping Milo with the case. Thanks to Alex's persistence, the murder of a psychologist and his girlfriend takes on new meaning. And Alex, never trained as a detective, is playing the role for all it's worth.

Anyone who has ever taken a class called Psychopathology or anyone who would ever contemplate it should check out Alex Delaware in *When the Bough Breaks*.

Sheri Kraft
Alibi Books, Glenview, IL

The Beekeeper's Apprentice by Laurie R. King (1993)

It's been years since I read this book and although I knew the general outline of the story I remembered very little detail. One visual image stuck with me over the years — very precise cuts in the leather seat of their carriage, the clue that led Mary Russell and Sherlock Holmes to their nemesis. I intended to skim the book and write this review but as I read I wanted just one more chapter, and then one more, and another until I closed the book with as much satisfaction as the first time I had read it. From the first words I loved this story. This second reading increased my enjoyment of it and my respect for King's authorship.

I had forgotten the charm, joy, sorrow and compassion that this story evokes. I had forgotten the humor and wit and the little jabs at the canon. I had forgotten that this is truly Mary Russell's story, not just another Holmes' pastiche. It is, after all, the narration of the beekeeper's *apprentice*.

Fifteen-year-old Mary Russell, walking with her nose in a book, literally stumbles across fifty-something Holmes on the Sussex Downs. It is 1915 and Russell has just lost her family in a car accident. She finds both challenge and comfort from Holmes, Mrs. Hudson and Dr. Watson. Holmes' intellectual match, Russell learns much under his tutelage. Together they solve the case of a landowner's odd illnesses and, with stunning heroism from Mary, rescue the kidnapped daughter of an American senator. Then off Russell goes to Oxford until a near fatal bombing on Holmes' doorstep and another at Russell's own door brings them together to find the person trying to destroy them. After several false starts, threats to their friends and family, and a judicious retreat, Russell unlocks the cipher cut into that leather seat — MORIARTY. And so the stage is set for a deadly battle. Thanks to Holmes' cunning and Russell's skill and courage they survive. And so we have the great gift of Russell's narrative.

Holmes purists howl at pastiches and parodies. We must respect their devotion, I suppose. But they are missing an incredibly good story here. And I pity them for that.

Kathleen Riley
Black Bird Mysteries, Keedysville, MD

Dark Nantucket Noon by Jane Langton (1975)

When you come home again at last, Mary, darling, here's what we're going to do. We're going to have a holiday on this island. I want to show you around. I want to gesture grandly like an Indian sachem or a First Purchaser or a Proprietor. I want to say "Lo! see where the boat comes in! Avast! here's where my tire went flat! Behold! a place to buy fried clams!"

Jennie and I planned our honeymoon based on *Dark Nantucket Noon*. It's a great guidebook, taking place throughout the island and describing all its important landmarks, natural and manmade. When we arrived, we saw just how well Jane Langton had captured every detail of this beautiful setting. I can't think of another writer who does more with her locations or takes better advantage of all they have to offer — not just in terms of geography, but the intellectual, cultural and political landscape as well. *Dark Nantucket Noon*'s chapter headings are taken from Herman Melville, and Langton describes the island's seafaring history. The tension between development and conservation runs through the story.

But what really got us excited about going to Nantucket is Langton's infectious enthusiasm. Some time ago in The Drood Review, I wrote: "Jane Langton is an utterly charming writer. If the sheer glory and rapture of her writing doesn't win you over, maybe it'll be the wit, the erudite observation, the perfect sense of place, the author's neat line-drawings, or most likely, the totally wonderful people: eccentric, normal, wise, stupid, self-assured, confused and usually all at once. One way or another, Langton will win you over." And as I've been rereading Langton this summer, I've again been struck dumb, in awe of everything she's done, everything she knows and everything she brings to life.

Dark Nantucket Noon is also a cunning and ingenious whodunit, a murder during a total solar eclipse that makes use of all that the occasion offers. Not all of Langton's books are whodunits; in her more recent work, we usually learn the killer's identity early on. But there remains plenty of suspense, and every entry in this long-running series (by far the longest-running current traditional mystery series) is a pleasure.

Jim Huang
Deadly Passions Bookshop, Carmel, IN

The Spy Who Came in From The Cold by John le Carré (1963)

Of how many books has it been said over the years that *this* one is unique, or *this* one started it all, or *this* is the one against which all others must be measured? And how often is it true?

Well, it's true for *The Spy Who Came in from the Cold*. Never again could an espionage novel be written without the writer, and the readers, being aware of the way in which this seminal novel forever changed spy stories.

Joseph Conrad's *The Secret Agent* and W. Somerset Maugham's *Ashenden* each have been credited with being the first modern spy novel, but it was John le Carré in this masterpiece who convinced readers that the good guys and the bad guys do the same things, for the same reasons, and all that separates us from them is that we're right and they're wrong.

Alec Leamas, a British agent, crosses the border into East Berlin with the intention of bringing into the West a former Nazi counterspy who will be able to provide valuable information. Already a disillusioned drunk, Alec and his lifestyle provide the perfect cover for getting into the Communist sector, where he is believed to be a defector.

When he is offered money to reveal secrets, he accepts, and soon learns that he has been used as a pawn to strengthen the position of former Nazi Hans-Dieter Mundt, now the head of the East German counterintelligence unit and a secret British double agent.

His escape over the Wall is arranged, but when he realizes that a girl he was taking with him was shot by his own colleagues because she was a security risk, he remains in the East to be killed as well, knowing that his life had been and would continue to be pointless.

The book, le Carré's third, was an immediate and enormous success, guaranteeing the author's position on bestseller lists for the next four decades.

An excellent film was made in 1965, starring Richard Burton and Claire Bloom, but its unrelenting bleakness prevented it from becoming a box-office success.

Otto Penzler
The Mysterious Bookshop, New York, NY

To Kill a Mockingbird by Harper Lee (1960)

I can't think of *To Kill a Mockingbird* without remembering Mary Badham and Gregory Peck. I always liked the book, but it was the movie that made it unforgettable. It was the first old (to me — I was twelve, okay?) movie I really liked, one that felt timeless and immediate even though it was about events states and decades away.

That's why two things always surprise me when I reread the book. The first is how faithful the movie is, how perfectly the actors and script tell Harper Lee's story. The other is that the book is still — and this is no criticism of the movie — better.

There are no significant differences — all the events and major characters are in the movie — but the book has room for the details of small town life. Lee constantly presents short but vivid portraits of Mr. Merriweather, the "faithful Methodist under duress," or Tyndal's Hardware Co., where the motto is "You-Name-It-We-Sell-It."

That lively world is one of the reasons *To Kill a Mockingbird* has been taught in English classes for decades (it was one of the few exemplars of "good literature" that didn't bore me to tears in high school). It also makes this book one of the first and best historical mysteries ever written — for it is most definitely a mystery.

The most obvious mystery element is the trial of Tom Robinson. This is more legal thriller than deductive mystery, but Atticus' courtroom skills certainly uncover the truth of what happened on the night of November the 21st. The real mystery, however — the one that is most satisfyingly resolved — is "Who is Boo Radley?"

It's not a conventional puzzle, but then again Scout is not a conventional heroine. Her fascination with Boo Radley drives the story, and its climax is her simple acceptance of him ("'Hey Boo', I said."). It's a human mystery story, and that warm humanity is why *To Kill a Mockingbird* transcends so many of the genre's boundaries.

Chris Aylott
Space-Crime Continuum, Northampton, MA

Darkness, Take My Hand by Dennis Lehane (1996)

For years, I've visualized a friend of mine as Spenser. His name is Tom; he has Spenser's build, charm, and unflinching morals. But as we've both grown older, Tom has changed places in my mind, becoming my mental image of Dennis Lehane's Patrick Kenzie.

I'm not sure Tom appreciates the role. He likes the character, but Kenzie lives in a messy world. Kenzie gets folded, mangled and stapled on a regular basis, and he's frequently powerless while bad things happen to his favorite people.

Kenzie has a lot in common with Spenser. He's a Boston private eye, flippant and tough, determined to do the right thing whatever the cost. He has more roots than Spenser, though — Lehane has carefully detailed Kenzie's past, exploring the influences that his childhood friends and abusive father have had upon him. He's closely tied to the Dorchester neighborhood he grew up in, and has none of Spenser's timelessness.

Because his roots are so important to him, Kenzie isn't the kind of self-contained crusader who can walk into a situation, fix it, and walk away without a backward glance. He feels, and the corruption of the world has a deep impact on him.

Does this make him a better character than Spenser? Possibly. Flawless knights in shining armor get old after a while. Their unswerving rightness makes them too self-satisfied for their own good.

Kenzie cares too much to be complacent. He's vulnerable to evil, and his vulnerability makes his heroism that much more exciting.

All this correctly implies that *Darkness, Take My Hand* is heavy reading. There are light moments — Lehane has a wicked sense of humor, and the banter between Kenzie and his partner Angela Gennaro is as smart and witty as it comes. But this book is a dark entry in an intense series, and Lehane himself has said that he warned his mother not to read it.

Dennis Lehane's books are not for everyone. But when you're too old for flawless heroes, Patrick Kenzie is refreshingly human.

Chris Aylott
Space-Crime Continuum, Northampton, MA

Get Shorty by Elmore Leonard (1990)

Elmore Leonard doesn't really write mysteries. He writes Crime Caper novels. Humorous Crime Caper novels. Laugh-out-loud Humorous Crime Caper novels. And *Get Shorty* is one of his best.

A South Florida snowbird who lives in a Detroit suburb, Leonard sets his capers in Detroit, or Miami, or both. I once had a customer in my store who told me he went to public school in Detroit with Leonard, and that Leonard used the names of his Detroit school buddies in his novels. (I think he said his name was used in *Stick* or *La Brava*.)

Leonard's capers are about small time crooks, criminals and shylocks. Not the top brass Don Corleones of the gangster world, but the average Joe street guy, who strikes it big, or tries to. Sometimes they pull it off, and sometimes they don't. But you're always rooting for them as the underdog.

Get Shorty is a novel within a movie within a novel. The plots are all subplots, and the double crosses are triple crosses. And once you're done reading it, you realize that you, the reader, have been had!

Chili Palmer is working the streets and keeping a book for a Miami loan shark named Momo. Collecting on an overdue payment from a dry-cleaner with a heavy gambling addiction,

Chili finds himself in Hollywood, in the middle of the movie business, pitching his real life story as a shylock to actors, producers, and studio heads. In the process, Chili outsmarts the producer, out-deals his gangster boss, and double-deals his oldest enemy. And manages to come out at the end with the girl! Gotta love this guy, and this book.

As a crime-caper, *Get Shorty* is one of the best. And it has our vote for the Best Last Line Award: "Fucking endings, man, they weren't as easy as they looked."

Joanne Sinchuk
Murder on Miami Beach, North Miami Beach, FL

Sleeping Dog by Dick Lochte (1985)

For a first novel, *Sleeping Dog* not only braves a risky concept, it displays rare control. The idea of a detecting team — more often a detective and a narrator/interpreter — is as old as the genre. What Dick Lochte does is play with the form by having each detective, aging private eye Leo Bloodworth and precocious teen Serendipity Dahlquist, tell the tale. The conceit is that each has written a book about the case and rushed to publication, leaving the savvy house acquiring both manuscripts to combine them in a single volume. This allows the reader to see the case not as mirrored, but from different, often contradictory, perspectives. Lochte is able to leak in information, occasionally foreshadowing, sometimes revising, what we think we know. Thus he gains extra tension — and opportunities for humor. It's a very difficult balancing act: keeping both voices true; keeping his face straight. This is even more fun when he salts the situational humor with riffs on the genre, welcoming the reader as a savvy partner in the joke.

Serendipity to Leo: "*...When a man's partner is killed, he's supposed to do something about it. It doesn't matter if he liked him or not, he's supposed to do something about it," I quoted from one of my favorite old movies.*

Or, earlier, Leo to Serendipity: "*That happens when you've been dead awhile. Rictus. Some writer called it 'the ivory grin' which may be a little melodramatic but says it all."*

The case begins when Serendipity's dog is snatched and, reluctant to lose this one memento of her dead father, she skates across town to hire Leo "the Hound" to find Groucho. The crusty PI seems already to have stepped into some caca because of his slimy partner. These story tracks then run along past the girl's appalling family, the Mexican mafia, some ancient history, some modern mayhem, and what can only be the Hollywood/Los Angeles culture, to a surprise convergence. Could the journey have been shortened a bit, tightened? Sure, but credit Lochte with finding a winning balance between humor and violence and for brilliant characterization as well as knowing LA inside out.

Barbara Peters
The Poisoned Pen, A Mystery Bookstore, Scottsdale, AZ

Rough Cider by Peter Lovesey (1986)

Peter Lovesey was the recipient of the 2000 Cartier Diamond Dagger Award from the Crime Writers Association, and winner of the CWA Gold Dagger in 1983 for *The False Inspector Dew*. *Rough Cider* was out of character for him at the time. From 1970 he had written a several novels set in Victorian England featuring Sergeant Cribb and Constable Thackeray. These are constructed along classical lines, borrowing from the principals of traditional mystery. Lovesey would go on to write several books featuring Bertie, Prince of Wales, and Peter Diamond, Bath CID.

Rough Cider partakes both of the historical and the contemporary. During the waning years of World War II, the discovery of a skull in a barrel of Somerset cider leads to the hanging of Duke Donovan, a US serviceman. Nine-year-old Theo Sinclair, recently evacuated from London, is the prosecution's primary witness, and his recollections of the events leading up to the murder are the subject of the novel. Twenty years pass. Dr.

Theo Sinclair, now a university lecturer, is visited by Duke Donovan's daughter Alice who has reason to believe that her father was unjustly convicted. She persuades Sinclair to join her in her pursuit of what she thinks may be the truth, and they set out for the old cider farm — and a trip into Theo's memories and through the characters who people his past and have survived into the present. As they walk paths virtually unchanged over time, they scare up some more dangerous personalities who refuse to stay put.

Lovesey's singular talent is in a seamless blending of character and setting, motivation and plot. He can create the very best of mysteries by creating doubts out of apparent certainties, disrupting the landscape even as he reestablishes faith in his protagonists. On more than one occasion, *The False Inspector Dew* has been saluted as Lovesey's best work, paying homage as it does to the classical mystery novel while incorporating memorable characters and delightful bits of humor. But *Rough Cider* is justly celebrated for incorporating a more contemporary mystery form, merging the psychological and suspenseful nature of character into the problem-solving genre.

Kathy Phillips
Spenser's Mystery Bookshop, Boston, MA

The Deep Blue Good-by by John D. MacDonald (1964)

What makes a book a classic is not the money it makes, or how many bestseller lists it is on, or who is reading it, but rather its timelessness, its ability to endure. When we go back to read some of the older books we once loved, we are immediately struck by how old they are, and how dated. Well, we think, they are still very good books, just excellent examples of that era. When I started to reread *The Deep Blue Good-By*, I fully expected to be brought back to the era of the sixties, since the book was written in 1964 and I first read it in the 1970s.

Boy, was I wrong! Travis McGee is as much a 21st century man as any I've met. I was in love with him thirty years ago, and

I am in love with him all over again now. Every scrap of dialogue, every character description, every plot he gets into, are all still fresh, modern and up-to-date. I can see him standing there in front of me as vividly now as in 1964. His philosophies, which John D. MacDonald sprinkles liberally throughout the books, are still appropriate (and true!). The Travis McGee series of books are truly classics in every sense of the term.

All the Travis McGee books have the same plot. A friend of his (usually female), or a friend of a friend (also usually female), has a wrong done to her involving a sum of money. Travis, who lives on a houseboat, the Busted Flush, moored in slip F-18 at Bahia Mar yacht basin in Fort Lauderdale Harbor, is taking his retirement a little at a time, and when he needs money, earns it as a salvage expert. Which means if you have "lost" something, usually cash, he "finds" it and reclaims it for a fee of 50%. While finding the lost article, he meets and defeats the bad guys, and always, always, always gets the girl. I understand this perfectly, because he always gets me.

Joanne Sinchuk
Murder on Miami Beach, North Miami Beach, FL

The List of Adrian Messenger by Philip MacDonald (1959)

There may not be another mystery that centers around words and language to the extent that *The List of Adrian Messenger* does. Clues include the strict definition of the word conspiracy, the proper spacing after a semicolon, the correct pronunciation of a family name, and the way a Frenchman understands the last words of an Englishman. But the most important words are the question Adrian Messenger asks about the ten men on a list he gives his friend George Firth: "Are these men living at these addresses?" A seemingly innocuous question, but Messenger dies within a day of asking it. Soon after, Scotland Yard discovers the pertinent question is "Are these men *living* at these addresses?" With Messenger dead, our sleuths have to discover what the ten men and Adrian have in common and whether a string of seemingly unrelated accidents could really have been the work of a serial killer.

Like all of Philip MacDonald's mysteries, this is a traditional British whodunit, containing a little romance, a lot of logic and plenty of suspense. MacDonald tells us that the story is set "... somewhere between the Second World-War-To-End-World-Wars and the yet-to-come Third which, by eliminating mankind altogether, will really do the trick ..." The story stands up to the test of time quite well. The clue concerning a typewriter may puzzle some younger readers, who have never used anything except a word processor. And I could wish that the most prominent female character, Adrian's sister-in-law Jocelyn, had a little more sense when it comes to love. But the murderer's schemes and disguises would work in any era.

Jennie G. Jacobson
Deadly Passions Bookshop, Carmel, IN

The Chill by Ross Macdonald (1964)

A masterpiece on many levels, *The Chill* stands out among Ross Macdonald's series of Lew Archer detective novels. Such unobtrusive yet important details as the fog that sweeps in throughout the first half of the novel indicate Macdonald's amazing ability to manipulate the feelings of the reader, and are often key elements in pulling you further into the story.

Things begin when Archer is hired by a newlywed husband to find his wife, who disappeared the day after they were married. Archer locates her easily, but what begins with a disappearance in a small town soon escalates into an investigation of three different murders spanning twenty years. Everyone Archer comes into contact with has a role to play in the unfolding drama, and the plot takes so many twists that it's easy to become disoriented. However, Macdonald handles the many threads like an expert weaver and leaves you still putting the pieces together five minutes after you finish it.

Unlike earlier writers of the pulp detective story, Macdonald finds it easy to avoid one-dimensional characterization. And rather than writing a classic crime novel in which it is difficult to like anyone, Macdonald goes in the opposite direction, creating characters whose very flaws make them sympathetic. It is easy for the reader to understand why Archer often feels bad that he can't always help everyone he meets.

With *The Chill*, Macdonald managed to combine the skillful plotting of Dashiell Hammett and the beautiful atmosphere of Raymond Chandler into a book that surpasses both in terms of sheer, gripping readability. Yes, this is one of those books that you end up staying awake half of the night to finish, and I can't think of a better reason to be awake until three o'clock in the morning.

Andrew Necci
Creatures 'n Crooks Bookshoppe, Richmond, VA

Bootlegger's Daughter by Margaret Maron (1992)

It was an old crime and one that went unsolved. Eighteen years earlier Janie Whitehead was found bludgeoned and shot in an abandoned mill, her three-month-old baby screaming beside her. The case rocked Colleton County, North Carolina. Now that baby is ready for college and she desperately wants to know what really happened in that mill. Who better to approach than her former baby-sitter, Deborah Knott, now a lawyer, a Democrat, and a woman with serious spine?

Deborah already has enough going on in her life. A blatant case of judicial racism has convinced her to set her sights on a judgeship. As the youngest child and only daughter of Kezzie Knott, the county's most notable bootlegger, Deborah has more than a few strikes against her in the race. Besides the moonshine connection, she's a woman and a white candidate running against an admirable black contender. And that's before the smear campaign begins and the murderer strikes again.

The novel is thick with characters: hot and cold running relatives, conniving colleagues, and intriguing men — after all,

Deborah's thirty-four and single. But despite its gripping plot, the strength of the story lies in the place. Margaret Maron immerses us in the new South: we smell the jasmine, taste the corn muffins, nod to the gentry, and elbow our way through the festive crowds at political fundraisers. We feel the rising tension as simmering secrets begin to bubble up. Deborah's not afraid of issues and encounters plenty in the course of unravelling the mystery. And the author is gutsy enough to leave Deborah and her readers with an ethical conundrum at the end.

Margaret Maron was already well established in the mystery world with her Sigrid Harald police procedurals when she broke new ground and introduced Deborah Knott. That year *Bootlegger's Daughter* scooped the awards. And rightly so.

Mary Jane Maffini
Prime Crime, Ottawa, Canada

Death of a Peer by Ngaio Marsh (1940)
(aka Surfeit of Lampreys)

Ngaio Marsh is known for her excellent prose, her memorable characters, and her gruesome murders. All of these elements are present in *Death of a Peer*, where the rich and odious Lord Wutherwood is dispatched by means of a skewer through the eye, and the chief suspects are the family of his brother Lord Charles, the charming and impoverished Lampreys.

I've always loved the original title of this book: *A Surfeit of Lampreys*. I like the way it sounds, but I also admire its witty commentary on the title characters, and even its ambiguity. Who, exactly, are the surplus Lampreys? Are they the murder victim (also a Lamprey) and his very peculiar wife? Or does the title refer to members of the sympathetic Charles Lamprey brood, who cheerfully live beyond their means, and are always saved at the brink of financial disaster by some fortuitous circumstance — in this case the violent death of their rich relative?

I'm amused, also, by the name Marsh chose for the family that she paints in such loving detail. My dictionary defines a lamprey as "an eel-like, parasitic, jawless fish." An appropriate and witty commentary on the fictional Lampreys and all that they represent, but surely a trifle insulting to the real-life friends who served as their model.

Ngaio (pronounced "nye-o") Marsh's series characters, Chief Detective-Inspector Alleyn and Inspector Fox, are present to solve the crime, but are not well fleshed out, and alas, Alleyn's wife, Troy, plays no part in this book. The story is mostly seen through the eyes of Roberta Grey, a young friend who is visiting the Lampreys. The first two chapters, which describe Roberta's friendship with the family in her native New Zealand and how she came to visit them in England, are strongly autobiographical (see Marsh's autobiography, *Black Beech and Honeydew*).

It is the story of the Lampreys, with their real life connection to the author, rather than the mystery story itself, that distinguishes *Death of a Peer* as one of our 100 Favorite Mysteries of the Century.

Karen Spengler
I Love a Mystery, Mission, KS

Sadie When She Died by Ed McBain (1972)

Sadie When She Died by Ed McBain is the twenty-fifth book in the 87th precinct series. This year McBain published the fiftieth in the phenomenal series.

A week before Christmas a call comes into the squad room of the 87th precinct from a man named Gerald Fletcher who reports that he has just arrived home from a business trip to find an intruder in the midst of attacking his wife. When Steve Carella, the detective on duty, arrives, he finds that the intruder is gone and the wife has been eviscerated. While being interviewed by Carella, the husband makes a very strange statement: "I'm delighted someone killed her." Soon after this a junkie confesses to the murder and the case is closed. Carella can't get the husband's statement out of his thoughts, and even though the junkie has confessed, Steve thinks that the husband did it — and Fletcher is daring the policeman to arrest him for the murder. Hunches are great in police work, but proof is a necessity. Carella sets up surveillance on Fletcher, through which the men of the 87th learn the truth — and it is very bleak indeed.

Ed McBain's 87th precinct novels are the best police procedurals written at any time. He includes the weather and the city as very important parts of the story. Every time I read an 87th precinct mystery I feel as if I have had a letter from an old friend bringing me up to date on what they have been doing. From *Cop Hater* (1956) to *The Last Dance* (2000) this is for my money some of the best storytelling around.

Paige Rose
Mystery Loves Company, Baltimore, MD

The Sunday Hangman by James McClure (1977)

I remember reading the James McClure books in the 1970s and being blown away by his detailed description of South Africa under the lash of apartheid rule. *The Sunday Hangman* is a perfect example of his craft, of weaving the little bits of everyday life of South Africa into a complex mystery about an avenger-murderer who is going around the country hanging people with almost professional skill.

Tromp is an Afrikaans police inspector who is very disrespectful of nearly everybody, except his bright Bantu assistant, Zondi. Tromp can't let anyone know how much trust he places in Zondi, who is supposed to be just a gofer and is always referred to as "your boy." When a body is found a rural district, the police realize that various hangings around the Natal are not suicides but clever murders. The investigation takes Tromp and Zondi to the slums of Durban, black shanty towns, as well as the remote countryside filled with truculent Afrikaans farmers. One of the most memorable scenes is the encounter with the gorgeous, sexy 15-year-old daughter of one of the farmers, all told in about four paragraphs — but four pretty exotic paragraphs.

McClure tells the story with vivid economy. Sometimes you have to reread a line or two to understand that some crucial piece of information has been presented. He allows his characters to be revealed by what they do and say, rather than with long descriptions. And the setting in this country struggling to oppress a huge majority of its population is simply fascinating. Little details such as the beaten dirt floor of Zondi's house where his wife has drawn lines in the dirt to replicate wooden planks, make you feel you are there. All McClure's books should be available to readers, and *The Sunday Hangman* is one of the best.

Pat Kehde
The Raven Bookstore, Lawrence, KS

If Ever I Return, Pretty Peggy-O by Sharyn McCrumb (1990)

If Ever I Return, Pretty Peggy-O is the first book in Sharyn McCrumb's lyrical portrayal of Appalachia, known as the Ballad series. The author has studied Appalachia and its ancient ballads for many years and shows their continuous evolution in her novels. *Peggy-O* introduces us to Sheriff Spencer Arrowood, a gentle man who has a deep understanding of human nature and an abiding love for Hamelin, his small Tennessee town. Plans are afoot for the class of '66 high school reunion when a 1960s folk singer, Peggy Muryan, moves to town. Once quite famous, her popularity has declined, and she seeks solitude to write songs for a comeback

When Peggy receives a postcard reading, "IS LITTLE MARGARET IN THE HOUSE OR IS SHE IN THE HALL" she recognizes it as both lines from a ballad she sang and an anonymous death threat. Sheriff Arrowood dismisses it as a prank until an animal is killed and mutilated with the symbol of a Vietnam-era army unit.

Against a background of ancient ballads and 1960s folk and rock music, the author delineates the seminal events that formed a generation. She writes, "you could divide the women of the class into Mary Tyler Moore and Mrs. Peel. They had lived on the cusp of an era, when Beaver Cleaver went out and Eldridge Cleaver came in, and nobody quite knew what to do about it." The men either went to Vietnam or didn't.

McCrumb is unusual because she writes complex plots, leaves fair clues, brings characters to life, and evokes a sense of place rarely equalled in modern literature. Preceding the Ballad series but still continuing is a lighter, funnier series about Elizabeth MacPherson. From these well written, lighthearted stories, the author's writing has evolved into the more serious and ethereal ballad tales, but the humor has not been lost. Watching the growth of an author over a period of more than twenty years is a rare pleasure. As the Ballad books continue, the kudzu vines grow evermore entangled, and the author's love and deep knowledge of Appalachian traditions and music grow more enticing.

Anne Poe Lehr
Poe's Cousin, White Plains, NY

A Stranger in My Grave by Margaret Millar (1960)

Though she was often overshadowed and, late in her career, outsold by her husband, crime writer Ross Macdonald, Margaret Millar was a more original and creative writer than her famous spouse. Millar had the gift of taking the seemingly ordinary routines of daily life and finding the sinister undercurrents just beneath the surface.

Young wife Daisy Harker has a comfortable relationship with her husband Jim, at least until the odd nightmares begin. She dreams that she died four years ago, a dream that is terrifying in its realness. Daisy feels her life fragmenting, especially when she finds the grave of her dreams in the cemetery with the date of death the one she had dreamed. But there is a stranger's name cut in the stone instead. As Daisy feverishly tries to sort out what's happening to her, her cozy little world shifts around her. In a Millar novel evil lurks behind a bland face and terror stands waiting in the bright light of a beautiful day.

Millar wrote several tours-de-force in her career, including the often-imitated Edgar-winning novel, *Beast in View*, the stunningly prescient *How Like An Angel*, and the subtly unsettling *Beyond This Point Are Monsters*. She rarely has received due recognition for her achievements, but Margaret Millar is one of the most provocative and original crime writers of the century.

Dean James
Murder by the Book, Houston, TX

Devil in a Blue Dress by Walter Mosley (1990)

I would try to look innocent while I denied what they said. It's hard acting innocent when you are but the cops know that you aren't.

Walter Mosley has my heart. More particularly, Easy Rawlins has it. In this first Rawlins novel, Mosley produces an accidental private investigator who loves his little home and his simple life. When he gets mixed up in what seems to be an innocent search and find, his true talents begin to come to the surface, very slowly. Rawlins just wants to be left alone, but since he's out of a job and has a mortgage to pay, he takes up with some decidedly slimy critters. Only through careful and diligent desire to survive does Rawlins begin to get tough. Mosley shows us that Easy has nothing against human faults. For example, when he gets surrounded by a group of young punks who want to pick a fight, Easy just stands back and tries to be inconspicuous. It is only when his associate scares them away that Easy admits the reason he didn't want to take them on is that he doesn't "kill children." This is his way throughout the whole book, and indeed the whole series. He is the strong, silent type who keeps to himself but holds his own.

Fans of Raymond Chandler or Loren Estleman will love Easy Rawlins' take on the world. There are people to love and people to hate wildly here, and a respect for Easy that is unbending. He just wants to do his own thing, with his Easy style.

Ann Saunders
Murder, Mystery & Mayhem, Farmington, MI

Edwin of the Iron Shoes by Marcia Muller (1977)

Did Marcia Muller start it all? You know, the first contemporary female private investigator — smart, professional, strong, liberated. Okay, Sharon McCone wasn't the absolute first female PI writer — Maxine O'Callaghan's Delilah West appeared in a short story in 1974. But Marcia's *Edwin of the Iron Shoes* debuted in 1977 as the first full-length novel and preceded the first books by Maxine, Sue Grafton and Sara Paretsky by a slim margin, giving Marcia the undisputed number one title.

With over twenty Sharon McCone novels published in over twenty years, trying to choose one book to include in this list was a daunting task. Yet not to include one was unthinkable.

In rereading *Edwin*, I can only marvel at Muller's early work and see that even in the beginning her writing was suggestive of what might be coming. For instance: "Hank was almost as tall as the other man but next to him he looked gawky, as if his long limbs were fastened together at the joints with paper clips." What a fantastic mental picture that calls to mind. In the tenth book, *The Shape of Dread*, just when you think you've got it all figured out, Marcia peels away another layer and you're wondering what's next? Walking down McCone's mean streets of San Francisco, feeling her definite belief in righting wrongs, usually for the underdog, sharing in the relationship between

Sharon and her soul-mate Hy Rapinsky, all leave me thinking this is a woman I'd truly like to know. This is someone I'd want on my side in any situation.

Muller stretches the genre, always pushing the envelope in ways that only a handful of writers are capable of achieving. She modestly says, "I have a low threshold for boredom. And if I'm bored, then I know the reader will be also."

I doubt Marcia Muller could bore us even if she really tried. We hail her first book as one of the best of the century, and pay a tribute to a strong, smart, professional twenty-first century female author. Muller's legacy to the genre can not and will not be ignored.

Jan Grape
Mysteries & More Online, Austin, TX

Death's Bright Angel by Janet Neel (1988)

Death's Bright Angel is a stunning first novel that won the CWA John Creasey Award for best first novel. This novel is a brilliant vignette of business in Margaret Thatcher's England in the late 1980s. We are introduced to Francesca Wilson, who is on the fast track in the Department of Trade and Industry (where the author worked for 13 years), and to John McLeish of the London Metropolitan Police. Francesca is the eldest child and surrogate mother to four younger brothers, all of whom are musically gifted. Janet Neel's talent for characterization captures the eccentricities of Francesca's family and relationships while bringing McLeish's fiery emotions vividly to life.

The plot revolves around the murder of a manager of a failing textile factory in Northern England. What appears to be a simple fatal mugging immediately arouses McLeish's suspicions. The company seeks aid from the Department of Trade and Industry, which brings John and Francesca together — and the sparks begin to fly. Vivid descriptions of the half-empty textile factory bring home the desperate state of northern British industry under Thatcher's government. An American is interested in acquiring the factory but the Trade office is nervous about foreign involvement. I felt that the author was very clever to use Americans as an example of the rampant xenophobia towards foreigners and immigrants during these years. This novel is an excellent example of how the mystery genre is often the truest reflection of any given society at any given time.

I was captivated by Neel's ability to bring characters to life, paint each scene with fine detail, and create an intriguing plot. Neel also cleverly uses the music in Francesca's family to frame the plot. She is clearly at home in factories, the Board of Trade and the world of music. As a bonus she gives us a time capsule of a controversial and often painful era. I visited England during this period and was struck by the sudden disappearance of persons of color from the Underground and by the poverty in the North. This is a novel to be savored for its beautiful use of language, dazzling characterizations and tantalizing plot.

Anne Poe Lehr
Poe's Cousin, White Plains, NY

Mallory's Oracle by Carol O'Connell (1994)

Sergeant Kathleen Mallory is one of the most, if not *the* most, unusual police detectives to come along in the world of mystery fiction. Intelligent and headstrong, Mallory follows no rules but her own in the pursuit of truth. Her past is shrouded in mystery and she probably never had a real childhood. Willetta Heising in *Detecting Women III* describes Mallory as a "lone-wolf investigator." She does not want to be dependent on anyone's help in solving crimes and she comes off as cold and unfeeling. But from the first book I was fascinated with the character and I just knew that as her background was slowly revealed in succeeding books I was learning what drove Kathy Mallory to be the kind of person she was. This is a series that I hurry to read as soon as a new book arrives.

In *Mallory's Oracle*, she investigates the death of her adoptive father, Inspector Louis Markowitz. He and his wife, Helen, had taken in Mallory as a little street urchin. Now grown and more comfortable with computers than people, Mallory shows no emotion as she investigates her father's death. What does his murder have in common with the deaths of two elderly women? Mallory has to leave her safe world of computers to enter the shadowy world of people and their deceptions. She has to do what is the most difficult for her, work with others, in order to bring her father's killer to justice. *Mallory's Oracle* is followed by *The Man Who Cast Two Shadows, Killing Critics, Stone Angel* and *The Shell Game*.

Patsy Asher
Remember the Alibi Mystery Bookstore, San Antonio, TX

Child of Silence by Abigail Padgett (1993)

Abigail Padgett's Bo Bradley books are important for transcending the "mysteries with a message" subgenre. Padgett has been up-front about her motivations behind writing a mystery series in which the protagonist is someone living with a bipolar condition. However, the series resonates with the storytelling traditions of the Irish and Native American ancestors Padgett has gifted Bo with.

Child of Silence, set in San Diego, introduces readers to Bo's job as a child abuse investigator and the types of intuitive leaps and altered perceptions Bo can experience in the process of working on a case. When determining that the title character is deaf rather than retarded, Bo is applying her child welfare expertise. When she must work to decipher cryptic information resulting from his having witnessed a murder, she benefits from her occasional bouts of hyper-clarity. Like many contemporary detectives, Bo can sometimes be her own worst enemy, as she has to filter her data and analyze its merit in both manic and depressed stages, and as she bucks the system in her attempts to provide for children's welfare. Padgett also gives Bo a number of great supporting characters, including her antithesis of a boss, Madge Aldenhoven, who represents every by-the-book-and-the-outcome-be-damned bureaucrat.

Child of Silence, like many first novels, has a few flaws, but it deserves its place on the list as a sterling example of the way mysteries can not only present readers with a puzzle to solve and a modern day morality play, but also inform us of something outside our usual experience.

Maryelizabeth Hart
Mysterious Galaxy, San Diego, CA

Deadlock by Sara Paretsky (1984)

Amanda Cross once said that she had written her Kate Fansler series to help her keep her sanity and to give herself female images of a competent woman at a time in her life when she needed it. She said if she were starting a series now, she would like to think that she would have written the V.I. Warshawski series. Chicago-based V.I. Warshawski grew out of a similar need on Sara Paretsky's part.

Paretsky is an author whose books need to be read in sequence. She uses the entire series as a palette for developing and expanding V.I. — a professional PI who struggles with being independent while not isolated, being humane rather than legalistic and living up to her own feminist principles, no matter how risky or unpopular. Her best friend and mentor is an older woman and doctor committed to the same feminist principles.

Paretsky updates the image of the PI while simultaneously ushering us expertly into a world of institutional corruption, dramatically showing the consequences of maintaining the status quo. *Bitter Medicine*, for instance, involves the medical establishment and the abortion issue. *Killing Orders* revolves around corruption in the Catholic church. Later books cover societal treatment of the elderly (*Guardian Angel*), women in prison (*Hard Time*) and industrial pollution (*Blood Shot*).

Because of this, I think Sara has brought some of the freshest and most original ideas to series mysteries in this century. In

Deadlock, the second in the series, we meet the first of many of V.I.'s extended Polish family. Boom Boom Warshawski, retired hockey player for the Chicago Black Hawks, has met an accidental death on the shores of Lake Michigan. V.I., driven by family responsibility, thinks he was murdered and sets out to prove it. Drawing on her extensive knowledge of insurance and shipping (no wonder she was trying to maintain her sanity!), Paretsky delivers her most tightly plotted mystery.

Kate Mattes
Kate's Mystery Books, Cambridge, MA

Looking for Rachel Wallace by Robert B. Parker (1980)

This may be the perfect Spenser novel. It has everything his fans love about the series and explores the core of his character.

When radical feminist Rachel Wallace hires Spenser, he's at the peak of his powers and self-confidence. The bad guys don't give him much trouble in this adventure, and that's not particularly surprising. The real challenge is Rachel Wallace herself.

More accurately, it's her viewpoint that is the challenge. This book is all about the conflict between Spenser's white knight ethos and her feminist independence, and what drives Spenser up the wall is that she's right and he knows it.

Of course, this is a Spenser book, not a Rachel Wallace book. When she disappears, it takes every ounce of Spenser's legendary determination to find her. He goes through bad guys like the Terminator, beating clues out of each of them.

"I'm looking for Rachel Wallace" becomes his mantra, the phrase that focuses him on his task and turns him into an avenging angel. It is protectiveness taken deep into obsession. It even becomes a weapon, words that scare the truth out of his opposition by the way he says them.

The last half of the book seemingly vindicates the Spenser ethos — but that vindication is problematic when you consider it in the light of the first half.

In the first half, he is overprotective. He overreacts to several threats and attempts to handle situations that Rachel is perfectly capable of dealing with herself. He overdoes his job so badly that he gets fired — leaving Rachel vulnerable when the real threat appears.

Had Spenser been able to bend in the first half of the book, he probably wouldn't have needed his unbreakable will in the second half. His greatest strength becomes his greatest flaw.

Spenser dodges the bullet in *Looking for Rachel Wallace*. The good guys win. But the conflict between Rachel and Spenser exposes a crucial weakness in him, one that would lead to dark times in the books to come.

Chris Aylott
Space-Crime Continuum, Northampton, MA

The Club Dumas by Arturo Perez-Reverte (1996)

Arturo Perez-Reverte's *Club Dumas* is a postmodernist mystery, slyly acknowledging that the reader and the writer are accomplices in the fiction that has been created and in the entire mystery tradition. For me, it is that very acknowledgment of the process of suspending disbelief that makes the novel — especially its supernatural elements — work so well.

Perez-Reverte, a Spanish journalist, creates mystery novels that transcend many of the conventions of the mystery genre, while at the same time alluding frequently to these conventions.

His many references to Sherlock Holmes and to Agatha Christie, his protagonists who are solitary figures searching for truth, the wonderful conundrums that he proposes and solves, all demonstrate how masterfully he is manipulating the genre.

He also expands the genre by including so many arcane and wonderful bits of knowledge in his novels. In *Club Dumas*, it is both the information about Dumas *pere* and the sources for the Musketeer novels as well as the extensive book lore. In *The Flanders Panel* it is what we learn about chess and Flemish painting. In both, this esoteric background adds to the richness of his mysteries. In Spanish, one says *me encanta* — it enchants me — about something outstanding. This is how I feel about *Club Dumas*: *me encanta*.

Christine Acevedo
Clues Unlimited, Tucson, AZ

Vanishing Act by Thomas Perry (1995)

Jane Whitefield is one of my favorite characters. She calls herself a guide, but what she really does is make people disappear by giving them new lives. At the start of *Vanishing Act*, the first book in the Whitefield series, Jane helps a woman escape from her husband, a monster to be sure. Arriving home, she meets John Felker. Felker is an ex-cop turned accountant, and he is in a lot of trouble. Someone has made it look like he embezzled a half million dollars. Knowing there was no easy way to prove his innocence, Felker decided to steal some of the money he had supposedly embezzled and run. He also knew this meant he would have to disappear. A friend of his, Harry Kemple, had told John about the talents of Jane Whitefield. Kemple had also needed to disappear and five years ago, Jane made that happen. Now, Jane will help John Felker become John Young.

As they travel together, running from the embezzlers, Jane does her best to explain what it takes to become someone new. And at last, when John's new identification is ready, Jane turns him loose. Shortly after returning home, Jane learns that Kemple is dead. Also dead is the man who created Felker's new identification. Fearing for Felker's life, Jane sets out to find him. It is a decision that has lifelong repercussions for Jane.

In *Vanishing Act*, Thomas Perry introduces us to a world so dangerous that escape is necessary to survive. Fortunately, that world also has Jane Whitefield, an amazing woman filled with spunk, wisdom and compassion.

Sheri Kraft
Alibi Books, Glenview, IL

Crocodile on the Sandbank by Elizabeth Peters (1975)

I am so pleased to have the opportunity to recommend Elizabeth Peters' *Crocodile on the Sandbank*. I have been a fan of Peters almost as long as I have been reading mysteries. In *Crocodile*, we are introduced to Amelia Peabody and her future husband, Egyptologist Radcliffe Emerson (aka Father of Curses).

Amelia is not meek and demure as women were expected to be in this time period (1880s). She could be considered an early feminist; she certainly has strength of character. When we meet Amelia, she has just inherited a large sum of money from her father and leaves England to travel in Egypt where she meets and falls in love with her soon to be husband and life partner.

One of the great things about this series is that it has retained its strengths and charms to this date. The characters grow and change, and more characters are added as needed. Amelia has a lot of fun foiling pretentious people. There is a lot of humor. I especially like the interaction between Amelia and her family. I remember when Ramses (her son) was an obnoxious preteen. Thankfully, Peters has him grow up into a wonderful young man, although he is still a bit of a know-it-all. You find yourself getting involved with the characters more than in many books.

This is a series I periodically reread to refresh my memory of what has gone before. The author holds a Ph.D. in Egyptology, but you are never talked down to. If you have knowledge of the land of Egypt and its history, the books may mean more to you, but if not, you still can enjoy them as I do. The author also writes nonfiction under her true name, Barbara Mertz, and more suspenseful novels as Barbara Michaels.

Maggie Mason
Lookin for Books, San Diego, CA

One Corpse Too Many by Ellis Peters (1979)

Edith Pargeter published her first book, *Hortensius, Friend of Nero*, in 1936. Some thirty years later, using the pseudonym Ellis Peters, she wrote *A Morbid Taste for Bones,* the book that introduced Brother Cadfael, former knight turned monk at Shrewsbury Abbey. A wonderful medieval series was born, which ended only upon Peters' death after twenty Cadfael novels and one collection of short stories.

She returned to Cadfael with the events of 1138 and a grisly battle in Shrewsbury over the throne of England between King Stephen and Empress Maud. *One Corpse Too Many* begins with the battle and the execution by King Stephen of 94 prisoners. Cadfael is called to the castle to help prepare the dead for burial. He notices that there are 95 bodies, one of which he believes was murdered.

Peters romanticizes the twelfth century a bit by sparing us the vermin, body odor and offal that permeated town life. However, she is scrupulous about her historical facts. Modern readers can identify with Brother Cadfael even in this secular age because he was a worldly knight and crusader prior to taking his vows and does not appear to be overly pious. Peters herself, as quoted in the third edition of *Twentieth-Century Crime and Mystery Writers*, says "I have one sacred rule about the thriller. It is, it ought to be, it must be, a morality. If it strays from the side of the angels, provokes total despair, willfully destroys — without pressing need in the plot — the innocent and the good, takes pleasure in evil, that is unforgivable sin."

I thoroughly enjoyed rereading this book. I was struck by how each character, major or minor, appeared to be tested for goodness and honor. The author managed to present a lively, intricate plot and strong characterizations without becoming preachy despite her emphasis on morality.

Anne Poe Lehr
Poe's Cousin, White Plains, NY

Blue Lonesome by Bill Pronzini (1995)

Bill Pronzini published his first book in 1971 and it earned him his first Edgar nomination. Thirty years and six Edgar nominations later we have *Blue Lonesome*. Why this didn't earn another Edgar nomination is a question best asked of the nominating committee for 1995. It is his masterpiece. Granted *Shackles* is also a masterpiece, but that's another story for another list.

Blue Lonesome is a moody, atmospheric and brooding novel about betrayal, murder and redemption. Our hero, Jim Messenger (a name not chosen by chance, I suspect), "is a CPA who hates his job, loves jazz, and can't forget a woman he has seen eating at the Harmony Café ... when she commits suicide, he is driven to find out why."

The novel starts out in San Francisco and quickly moves to Nevada, where Messenger sorts through the facts and the lies and discovers that the woman he couldn't get out of his mind was carrying around enough baggage for three people.

Many of Pronzini's novels deal with the theme of an outsider who is placed in harm's way because he/she happens to be in the wrong place at the wrong time. Sound a bit like Hitchcock? Many of the novels deal with a stranger dropped into an alien environment and asked to cope. Sound a bit like *Bad Day at Black Rock*? All these elements come into play and work themselves out beautifully in a book that made the New York Times Notable Books List for 1995. To quote their review: "There is a sharp sense of place in this moody crime novel, which evokes even the inner landscape of the hero's mind. For all the spareness of its style, this is a rich study of alienated people and the big open spaces where they live."

Jim Messenger is — to paraphrase Raymond Chandler — the best man of his time and a good enough man for any time. He is a member of the fraternity.

Bruce Taylor
San Francisco Mystery Bookstore, San Francisco, CA

Cat of Many Tails by Ellery Queen (1949)

The character of Ellery Queen underwent several metamorphoses over the years, from Philo Vance-ish fop, to silly, lovesick Hollywood hack, to absentminded nice guy. *Cat of Many Tails* is both a novel with EQ as chief protagonist in a murder mystery, and about EQ the person. It also prominently features the City of New York as a character, and even though it was written several years before Ed McBain's 87th Precinct opened for business, fans will recognize familiar ground.

A serial killer is loose in New York during a record breaking heat wave. How the city reacts to this and how "the crowd" behaves is an integral part of the story. Each body is found with a silk cord tied around its neck, all seem unrelated to each other in any way, and the police are baffled. EQ is asked to look over the cases to see if he can spot something, anything, to help in the increasingly frightening situation. Clearly anyone at all could be the next victim as it is not known how or why each one is selected, and the mood of the city becomes increasingly tense as time and the number of bodies progress.

More manhunt than classic murder mystery, this psychological thriller eagerly embraces the then-still-young field of psychoanalysis, and carefully interweaves bits and pieces of theory into the story. Mixed along with the attempt to fathom the personality of the killer and reason why he/she kills (and to figure out who'll be next), is EQ's attempt to understand his own personality and the reasons why he detects. Suspenseful and with colorful characters and subplots plus a great finale, this is one of many excellent Ellery Queen novels and, in my opinion, is the very best one.

AbiGail Hamilton
Black Bird Mysteries, Keedysville, MD

No More Dying Then by Ruth Rendell (1971)

Ruth Rendell is arguably the best writer of contemporary

British mystery fiction of the past and present centuries. Although she writes both series and nonseries mysteries, her classic police procedural series set in the English countryside is the best in the genre. *No More Dying Then* is an early entry in this series featuring Chief Inspector Reginald Wexford of the Kingsmarkham CID and his second in command, Inspector Mike Burden.

The story centers on a missing five-year-old boy, and is complicated by Burden's agonizing struggle to cope with the recent premature death of his wife. The missing boy's mother is a divorced, second-rate actress whose casual parenting style belies her devotion to her son. She isn't even exactly sure when the boy disappeared because the child she was watching in a neighbor's field turns out to be another boy. When the other children tell her that her son hasn't been with them for several hours, she panics and phones the police.

Wexford's team uncovers reports of a strange man and a red Jaguar seen near the children in the past few months, while Burden investigates the mother, her ex-husband and their circle of theatrical friends. Wexford begins to suspect a connection between this case and the unresolved disappearance of a twelve-year-old girl a year ago.

Rendell's mysteries are my favorites because they provide the perfect blend of classic British mystery with in-depth character studies. *No More Dying Then* is an outstanding example of her work. The superbly well-crafted plotting is enhanced by her fascinating psychological explorations into the lives of her characters. Each one is a fully-formed three-dimensional person we know intimately by the end of the story. The doomed relationship between straightlaced Mike Burden and the bohemian mother of the missing boy is nicely juxtaposed with Burden's sudden rejection of his children and his wife's sister who is caring for them. This is a story you won't be able to put down and I can't recommend it highly enough for anyone who loves British mysteries as I do.

Susan Ekholm
A Compleat Mystery Bookshop, Portsmouth, NH

The Wrong Murder by Craig Rice (1940)

Although both the first hardcover and first paperback editions of *The Wrong Murder* proclaimed the book a "Jake Justus Mystery," it was John J. Malone, a short, cigar-smoking night-school law graduate, who eventually emerged as the star of the trio of sleuths (which also included press agent Jake's beautiful socialite wife Helene) who wisecracked and drank their way across Chicago looking for clues, booze and poker games in a dozen or so books.

If tightly constructed plots are your thing, then Craig Rice's madcap stories aren't for you, since it's the cast, not the plot, that's usually tight. When they aren't working (which is most of the time), you'll find our sloshed sleuths hanging out at Joe the Angel's City Hall Bar, often joined by members of the city's underworld or police force, including Inspector Daniel Von Flanagan (he added the "Von" so people wouldn't think he was just another Irish cop). He never wanted to be a cop and resents murderers because he's convinced that they kill only to annoy him, while Malone rushes to defend them — "the thought of anyone actually going to jail visibly upsets him."

Jokes and comic situations were far more important to Rice (born Georgiana Ann Randolph) than whodunit. In fact, our sleuths lose track of the murder they set out to solve in this book and end up solving another case, hence the title. But not to worry. Rice wasn't about to waste even the germ of a plot and *The Wrong Murder* was quickly followed by *The Right Murder*. And more jokes.

Tom & Enid Schantz
Rue Morgue, Boulder, CO

The Circular Staircase by Mary Roberts Rinehart (1908)

If you like ghost stories, you will love *The Circular Staircase*. The author creates the most classic of settings, a large handsome house named Sunnyside, set among the hills of rural

Connecticut, across the valley from the elegant Greenwood Golf and Country Club. A very independent, intelligent middle-aged woman and her niece and nephew move in while their townhouse in New York is being refurbished. But from their first day at the house there are strange noises, nervous servants, vague figures looking in the windows. Then a murder at the foot of the circular staircase precipitates a rapid unraveling of all that seems sound and solid in their lives.

Mary Roberts Rinehart uses her descriptive powers to create this world of privilege and suspicion, and uses delicate literary devices, such as foreshadowing and irony, to enhance the complex plot. Her protagonist, Rachel Innes, is so likable, so smart, so feisty with everyone from the police inspector to her two charges, that you love spending time with her. It is entirely remarkable that the book was written in 1908 and yet reads like a contemporary novel (with a few politically incorrect asides and, of course, everyone smokes). It is definitely not a period piece, but a compelling, spooky story about the skeletons in the closet of the very rich.

Pat Kehde
The Raven Bookstore, Lawrence, KS

Blood at the Root by Peter Robinson (1997)
(aka Dead Right)

Detective Chief Inspector Alan Banks started fighting crime in Yorkshire, England in 1987 when the first in the series, *Gallows View,* was published. Since that time, Peter Robinson, also hailing from Yorkshire but now living in Toronto, Canada, has nurtured Banks through ten more books.

The years have not always been kind to DCI Banks, meting out professional and personal setbacks, along with the numerous cases he's successfully solved. His children have grown and moved away from home, and in *Blood on the Root*, his relationship with his wife hits a crisis point. Even his job is on tenuous ground.

It starts with a body being found in an alleyway, a young male, hit over the head and viciously kicked to death. Since he was a member of a white power group, the investigation centers on an earlier pub-fight he had with some Pakistani lads. Their questioning leads to an outcry from the community, which in turn pumps up the pressure from above to wrap it up quickly.

While his team follows this line of investigation, Banks pursues a lead on his own, which takes him to Amsterdam for the weekend and a secret meeting with an undercover cop. Although this nets a link to the murder, it's the excuse his superior has been looking for to suspend him, especially since Banks won't reveal what's transpired for fear of compromising the cop. Loyal readers will be shocked but delighted with Banks' parting shot.

They'll also know that all is not lost, that he still has the support of some fellow officers, and that he'll solve the case. The ending, while exonerating Banks, does not immediately set all wrong things right in his life. But that's what sequels are about.

Peter Robinson's series is highly recommended and just keeps getting better. The writing is always strong but Robinson likes to expand his skills by exploring tangents that add new dimensions to his plots. And new readers to his growing audience.

Linda Wiken
Prime Crime, Ottawa, Canada

Strike Three You're Dead by R.D. Rosen (1984)

Mystery bookstores have a difficult time finding appropriate books that will interest the precocious young adult reader. This debut sports mystery more than satisfies these readers, while appealing to the most hard core aficionado as well. It contains all the elements: a good read with a good voice, great dialogue from distinctive characters and a unique setting.

After playing center field for the Boston Red Sox for five

years, Harvey Blissberg, the narrator, was left unprotected in the expansion draft. We find him playing for the Providence Jewels in their first season. After a night game, Harvey is the last player in the clubhouse when he discovers the murdered body of his roommate, relief pitcher Rudy Furth, in the whirl-pool. Harvey surprises himself by questioning the team's members, owners and administrative staff to find the murderer. Meanwhile he's playing his best baseball ever. With just the right balance between mystery and baseball, and a reluctant amateur sleuth vs. the slow-moving Providence police, Rosen introduces a sports character with a conscience, and a plot that satisfies any demanding puzzle-solver.

Rosen wrote three more mysteries featuring Harvey, and at least once a month this bookseller curses the fact that this excellent series is out of print.

Judy Duhl
Scotland Yard Books, Winnetka, IL

A Broken Vessel by Kate Ross (1994)

It's hard to choose a best book among Kate Ross' four novels — they are all pretty much perfect. Ross, a Boston lawyer, died too young, but left behind four wonderful mysteries that make any sensible reader long for more — luckily, they bear repeated rereadings. Her novels all feature the nineteenth century dandy, Julian Kestrel, and his faithful valet (and former pickpocket), the aptly named Dipper. The amateur detective work of Kestrel is especially plausible because Ross chose a time period when there was no real, coordinated police force.

Ross' setups and plots are among the best, ever. Rereading one of them only a few years after the first time I read it, I was struck by not only the number of clues, but the fact that all the very complicated story threads were tied up in a satisfactory fashion at the end of the book. Ross' encyclopedic knowledge of law and nineteenth century slang (some of it extremely colorful, my favorite being "forks" for hands), never overwhelm her story; the history lessons are merely the details in the narrative's fabric. The atmosphere is perfectly recreated and authentic.

Setting the history aside, these books can be read just for the great, pure mysteries that they are. With her mastery of clues and suspects Ross was definitely writing in the finest Golden Age tradition, but she was also able to achieve the depth of characterization and theme found in the best of her contemporaries. Julian Kestrel becomes more and more of a three dimensional character as these four novels progress, and some of the issues Ross touches on rival Anne Perry's for their gruesome, heartbreaking qualities.

I think what makes *A Broken Vessel* in particular so fine is the fact that in the first chapter Ross introduces nearly every element of her plot, but they are all so seemingly unrelated that the skein of clues seems far too tangled to ever be unraveled. The resolution is credible yet ingenious. Juggling so many elements so perfectly — history, solid character development, and wonderful mysteries — was a real act of grace on Ross' part. If we as readers regret her early death, we can at least savor the gems she left behind.

Robin Agnew
Aunt Agatha's, Ann Arbor, MI

Concourse by S.J. Rozan (1995)

There's a line in the penultimate chapter of *Concourse* about a girl and a cat that's so perfect it brings tears to your eyes. At the end of this engrossing, complicated and consistently surprising story, private eye Bill Smith's small gesture is just right. Smith has no illusions, and this isn't one of those "the good end good and the bad end bad" stories. Indeed, S.J. Rozan leaves us with real questions about who's good and who's bad; and she's sophisticated enough to understand that good isn't always done by those who are good — and vice versa. But she's a master of the right touch. Smith can't fix everything, but he knows enough to make a real difference in the right people's lives.

This is private eye fiction of the highest order. Smith's investigation of the death of a security guard at the Bronx Home for the Aged begins with a lot of questions. He goes in undercover, and enlists his sometime partner Lydia Chin to investigate from the outside. Together, they uncover more questions that take them far beyond Mike Downey's death to a set of interlocking circumstances — some clearly evil and corrupt, some questionably so, but all integral pieces of this extraordinary puzzle. When Smith realizes the full scope of what is going on in and around the Bronx Home, he engineers a resolution that's satisfying, but still leaves us with a lot to think about.

Concourse has a heart, too, and we're also left with vivid pictures of the community and its inhabitants, of a woman facing her declining years with grace and humor, a former gang leader trying to lead a new life, and an urban landscape that knows little beyond deprivation and exploitation.

In Smith and Chin we have two private eyes who struggle to make a difference, and struggle too to understand and coexist with each other. As you move beyond *Concourse*, you'll see there's a gimmick to this series: Bill narrates one book, Lydia narrates the next. Each brings different perspectives, different pieces to the puzzle. It's a relationship that challenges them, even as it dazzles us. Mysteries don't come any better.

Jim Huang
Deadly Passions Bookshop, Carmel, IN

Murder Must Advertise by Dorothy L. Sayers (1933)

I love a British mystery and I don't care much whether it's a cozy, a police procedural or downright hardboiled. In *Murder Must Advertise*, the queen of British mystery actually managed to blend elements of all three and created a cracking good mystery to boot.

Our hero, Lord Peter Wimsey, is asked to investigate a death at an advertising agency and becomes a copywriter in the firm. This is more than a simple mystery; we also get a good look at the advertising world of 1933, when the book was published. I was fascinated to find that not much has changed in nearly 70 years — the aim then, as now, was to convince me to buy a product or service I probably don't even want, much less need, and the ideas then were just as creative. Look for a particularly interesting comment about nicotine and remember that this was published in 1933, long before the dangers of nicotine became public.

So, off I go with Lord Peter, living a double life, snooping with a mischievous joy that had me waiting eagerly to see what he was going to do next. That's the charm of Lord Peter — he has so much fun detecting and yet he has a somewhat callous side that reminds me of some of the hardboiled detectives who want the world to believe they don't care about anything. Lord Peter is a man I would love to have as a friend.

Perhaps best of all, Sayers leads Lord Peter and me on a merry chase, with plenty of red herrings and enticing clues. One of the things I look for in a really good mystery is that the solution not be too easy and *Murder Must Advertise* satisfies that requirement better than most mysteries.

Lelia T. Taylor
Creatures 'n Crooks Bookshoppe, Richmond, VA

The Laughing Policeman by Maj Sjöwall & Per Wahlöö (1970)

From the great title to the complex character of the police inspector Martin Beck to the bizarre, nearly impossible crime, this is a great book. The title refers to a cop in the Stockholm force who is one among a dozen or so victims of a nasty mass murder, on a public bus in the middle of downtown Stockholm in the pouring rain! Martin Beck is the first of the many fictional police inspectors who are disenchanted with their personal life and with their inability to stem the tide of twentieth century urban evil. He has so many imitators in crime fiction that he seems familiar. But this series featuring Martin Beck began in the 1960s and was among the very first to present a cop who had a realistic private life and opinions about modern life and politics.

Beyond the marvelous character of Beck is the excellent description of dogged, methodical and very civil police procedure for tracking down the killer. The dialogue among the various policemen in Stockholm and their suspects is abrupt, amusing and revealing. The plot twists through quiet Swedish middle class life with some surprises to keep you guessing. First in the Martin Beck series is *Roseanna*; it is also very good. But *The Laughing Policeman* touches all the bases perfectly.

Pat Kehde
The Raven Bookstore, Lawrence, KS

Some Buried Caesar by Rex Stout (1938)
(aka The Red Bull)

Some Buried Caesar, the sixth novel about Nero Wolfe and Archie Goodwin, was Rex Stout's favorite. In it the two stars of this classic series shine.

Nero Wolfe, the massively rotund genius, has left his beloved brownstone to exhibit orchids at an exposition in upstate New York. Wolfe away from his natural environment is Wolfe at his most irascible and eccentric. Because he is desperate for a comfortable chair, he offers to investigate a grisly death by goring provided he can solve the crime in time to leave for home on schedule. He does, and in the process provides one of the great comic images in literature: Wolfe standing atop a boulder in the middle of a field, waiting to be rescued from an angry champion bull.

Vital to both solving the crime and to our tolerating the insufferable Wolfe is the smart, irreverent energy of Archie Goodwin. Handsome, athletic and quick with his fists, Archie is the leg man who gathers up witnesses and evidence for the reclusive Wolfe. His skepticism and wit make his narrative voice irresistible.

Another of Archie's specialties is handling women for Wolfe, who cannot abide them. The woman he handles in this case is Lily Rowan, the sly, beautiful heiress who becomes important in Archie's life. Archie's banter with Lily shows Stout's genius with dialogue. In one scene where Archie and Lily lunch together, their conversation has enough sexual sizzle to overcook their chicken and dumplings — all completely within the bounds of propriety.

One thing is missing in *Some Buried Caesar*: the household on West 35th Street, New York. Wolfe's carefully constructed universe there, complete with culinary wizard Fritz Brenner in the kitchen and orchid nurse Theodore Horstmann in the rooftop greenhouse, is an essential element in the series; knowing it helps to explain Wolfe's behavior in the outside world.

For that reason, a new Wolfe reader might want to begin with the first adventure, *Fer-de-Lance*, or with the trio of novels featuring Wolfe's archenemy Arnold Zeck *(And Be a Villain, The Second Confession, In the Best Families)*. Wherever you decide to begin the Wolfe saga, don't miss it. These books are the sort that convert literary snobs into happy mystery readers.

Karen Duncan
Seattle Mystery Bookshop, Seattle, WA

Brat Farrar by Josephine Tey (1949) (aka Come and Kill Me)

Josephine Tey was aptly called one of the "Queens of Crime" by Julian Symons in *The Murder Book*. Her crime novels have stood the test of time and *Brat Farrar* is a great example of her craft. Being on the Independent Mystery Booksellers Association list attests to its durability. Of the eight books Tey wrote, five were nominated for this list.

Brat Farrar was not Patrick Ashby, the long-lost missing twin believed to have committed suicide by drowning at age thirteen. Brat Farrar was a young man who loved working with horses, but couldn't get a job. If Patrick Ashby were alive, if Patrick had run away instead of drowning, Patrick would own the Latchetts stables. So Brat became Patrick. But Brat felt a strange kinship with young Patrick, and he certainly looked the part. He looked even more like the other twin, Simon, than Patrick ever had. He was shocked to realize early on that one member of the family didn't believe Brat was the prodigal son. So why had he been so easily accepted?

Certainly, Simon, the newly deposed heir to the estate, had no reason to allow him family status; others have their moments of doubt. Yet there he was, Brat Farrar, welcomed into the bosom of this family and accepted as one of their own.

Tey gradually builds her suspense, introducing the imposter, taking us into his mind, getting us to feel an empathy with him. As she presents the rest of the cast, the author causes us to doubt our certainty. Brat's quest of infiltrating the family changes from the con to the mission. Patrick's disappearance must be explained and his thirteen-year-old spirit must be avenged. Perhaps this stranger in their midst is the only one who can solve the mystery.

Henrietta Wilde
Whodunit? Mystery Bookstore, Winnipeg, Canada

Chinaman's Chance by Ross Thomas (1978)

While jogging on Malibu beach early one morning, Artie Wu trips over a dead pelican and sprains his ankle. He is helped by Randall Piers, a millionaire industrialist who walks along the beach every morning. Impressed by Artie and his partner Quincy Durant, Piers invites them to a party at his Malibu mansion. Piers is married to Lace Armitage, one of the Armitage sisters — the most popular folk singing group in the '60s. He hires Artie and Quincy to find his sister-in-law Silk Armitage, girlfriend of a local congressman who was recently murdered while investigating local corruption. Silk is hiding from the target of the congressman's investigation. Thus the virtuoso author Ross Thomas begins another complex mystery adventure.

Like peeling layers of an onion, Thomas gradually reveals that Artie and Quincy are working for a group of influential Washington insiders to prevent the mob from "redeveloping" the Southern California beach community of Pelican Bay. Pelican Bay, a "long grimy finger poked into the backside of Los Angeles" is controlled by the mob through an ex-CIA operative who double-crossed Artie and Quincy a decade earlier in Cambodia. As the story unfolds, we learn that everyone's past has a significant impact on current events. With classic Thomas surprises, Artie, Quincy, Otherguy Overby and Silk resolve the Pelican Bay situation to almost everyone's satisfaction.

Thomas is a master at developing unique characters and intricate plots that are completely believable. *Chinaman's Chance* is one of his best efforts. Artie and Quincy are also featured in *Out on the Rim* and *Voodoo, Ltd.*

John A. Hooper
Sherlock's Home, Liberty, MO

A Test of Wills by Charles Todd (1996)

This sophisticated first novel introduces shell-shocked policeman Ian Rutledge, a man who survived World War I's western front, but not without damage. Some is physical, the more serious is psychic. Rutledge is haunted by the cynical voice in his head that springs from Hamish, a young Scots soldier. Is Hamish just the voice of conscience? No matter, it is vivid, relentless: *"Ye'll no triumph over me!" Hamish said. "I'm a scar on your bluidy soul."* Hamish is also a great literary device, a way for a third person narrator to engage in dialogue that renders some aspects of his tale and his persona first-person.

Back at Scotland Yard in 1919 in an effort to salvage his

sanity, Rutledge runs afoul of a jealous superior. Bowles is overjoyed to hand him a loaded assignment: the murder of the well-liked Colonel Harris in his Warwickshire village. The political ringer: the chief suspect, Captain Wilton, is a much-decorated war hero and a friend of the Prince of Wales. He's also engaged to the Colonel's ward. A quarrel had blown up over the wedding just before Harris' death. The chief witness to Wilton's guilt is another former soldier, one despised for losing his nerve at the front, shattering life and reputation. Bowles has maliciously given Rutledge a no-win situation, though he cannot know the full resonance of the case for the beleaguered veteran.

Other suspects come into play as Rutledge moves painfully through his investigation. In the end, the reader realizes Todd has risked violating one of the tenets of detective fiction to reach an outcome that, along with the Hamish concept, has given some critics and readers pause. But not this one. I admire the imagination, the elegant writing, the convincing evocation of place and character, and the masterly style of the novice writer. And so did those who nominated it for the Edgar Award, the Creasey Dagger and other literary prizes.

Actually, what is ironic is that this writer is actually a pair of writers, mother and son, a piece of teamwork concealed until publication of their fifth series novel, *Legacy of the Dead*. It's the book where Rutledge visits Scotland and comes face to face with Hamish's home and family. More power to them that their collaboration is so seamless that no one discerned it.

Barbara Peters
The Poisoned Pen, A Mystery Bookstore, Scottsdale, AZ

Presumed Innocent by Scott Turow (1987)

Scott Turow's runaway bestselling first novel is perhaps best remembered for its clever plotting. Turow is a master of misdirection, using a full bag of tricks (starting with the title) to mask a series of clues as carefully — and fairly — laid as in an

Agatha Christie story, and unveiled with as effective a surprise. His magic includes diverting us with riveting suspense and complex psychological insights, and using our own sophistication as mystery readers to lure us into his trap. He even manages to make the fact that the narrator tells us he is deceiving us work to deepen rather than reveal the deception. The ultimate revelation of whodunit achieves that rare moment of epiphany present in only a handful of the greatest mysteries, when all the pieces of the puzzle are tossed in the air and reassembled, and the reader mentally reviews and recreates the entire story in a wholly new light, down to even a word-by-word reinterpretation of the hero's penultimate speech.

For all these fancy effects, though, Turow's truly outstanding virtue is his wizardry as a prose stylist: the ability to capture with elegance and precision the finest nuances of the human experience. In *Presumed Innocent*, he applies his dazzling skills to a present-tense narrative, giving this story of an attorney suspected of murdering his mistress a singular power and intensity. Readers will appreciate *Presumed Innocent* most if they tackle it after they are already familiar with the great mysteries of the Golden Age to which it pays such subtle homage — and when they have the time to read it straight through, panting and gasping all the way.

Jill Hinckley
Murder by the Book, Portland, OR

The Sands of Windee by Arthur Upfield (1931)

Although this novel was first published in 1931, the setting is 1925, in the state of New South Wales, Australia. Enter Detective-Inspector Napoleon Bonaparte, of the Queensland police. By his own declaration he is "the greatest detective Australia has ever known." Born of an Aboriginal mother and English father, he is in the vernacular of that time and place a half-caste. University educated with keen interests in a variety of subjects, he is unexpectedly appealing to all around him. His understanding of the beliefs and practices of the Aboriginies allows him to effectively move and work with them as well as whites.

The plot is wonderfully complex and meticulously developed. A white man has disappeared, leaving only an abandoned car. It is for Bony to discover or deduce what has happened two months later, with no clues and no body with which to work.

One of the joys of this book is the picture of life in Australia at that time, with a sense of the enormity of the land and the loneliness and privation of people trying to wrest a living from that hot, arid environment. Another joy is to watch Bony overcome the arrogance and condescension of the bigotry of racism.

Even seventy years later the narrative is clear, never stilted or preachy. And a pleasure it is to be spared the unending stream of vulgarities and obscenities that now often pass for contemporary dialogue.

Allen Hubin's crime fiction bibliography lists more than 40 Upfield titles, but beware: some were reprintcd with new titles. When you're lucky enough to find any, go ahead and read (and delight in) Bony's many guises and adventures.

B Jo Bauer Farley
Seattle Mystery Bookshop, Seattle, WA

The Ice House by Minette Walters (1992)

A body has been found on the grounds of an estate in a small English village. The three women living in the house are already vilified by the locals as well as the chief inspector for an incident that occurred years earlier, so they immediately become the target of some rough treatment. Red herrings abound in the search for the identity of the victim and killer and the story becomes more and more engaging as we are drawn into the psyches of the characters.

What makes this debut novel so interesting and unlike most other mysteries is the psychological studies woven throughout the story. The reader cannot help but consider the severe damage done by innuendo and gossip, both by one's neighbors and by the media, as well as the damage created by obsession. At the same time, we see the pain caused when a man is torn between professional duty and personal feelings.

To try to categorize this book would be an exercise in futility. It is neither cozy nor hardboiled nor police procedural. There's the element of good cop/bad cop. There's the small English village setting along with a rather grotesque description of the body. Minette Walters has created a unique blend of the many possible aspects of a mystery and is a welcome addition to my list of favorite authors.

Lelia T. Taylor
Creatures 'n Crooks Bookshoppe, Richmond, VA

Sanibel Flats by Randy Wayne White (1990)

When we first reviewed *Sanibel Flats*, we wrote that Randy Wayne White "hit the ground running" with what we assumed was his first novel, a thoroughly engaging action mystery introducing marine biologist Marion "Doc" Ford. Of course it turned out that White had written a number of paperback originals as Randy Striker and had been honing his writing skills for years, but that didn't diminish the impact of the debut Doc Ford novel.

It opens with the discovery of a body on Sanibel Island, where Doc is living quietly in a stilt house, collecting marine specimens for a biological supply company, drinking beer, and hanging out with his weird genius friend Tomlinson, a zonked out hippie with an amazing intellect and a decidedly mystical bent (who is loosely based on White's close friend Peter Mathiesson). Doc is a modern-day hobbit; he doesn't go looking for adventure, but it always finds him. Here he and Tomlinson journey to the cities and jungles of Central America, where at one point Doc finds himself umpiring a surreal baseball game in which one of the pitchers is a hot-headed revolutionary for whom Doc wisely calls a very wide strike zone. While it's widely assumed that Doc is a former spy, White actually gives very few details about either Doc or his past. About all we really know is that he wears glasses, has the instincts of a street fighter when in a tight situation, enjoys the company of women, and is happiest when he's on or near the water. White's intent was to make Doc a cipher in terms of his psychological and emotional makeup, but for us he comes across as a chivalrous, even altruistic character, fiercely loyal to his friends and forever determined to right wrongs and protect the people he cares for.

Many readers consider Doc to be a modern-day Travis McGee. Not being great fans of that series ourselves, we are grateful for the wry asides that replace the interminable sermonizing in the McGee series and for the absence of McGee's paternalism toward women. White, a great storyteller in person, never forgets that his first goal as a writer is to entertain the reader, and we find his books so endearing that we're willing to forgive his occasional political incorrectness.

Tom & Enid Schantz
Rue Morgue, Boulder, CO

I Married a Dead Man by Cornell Woolrich (1948)

Although my bookshelves are expectedly crowded with mysteries, most of the space is actually taken up by various volumes of fairy tales. *I Married a Dead Man* appeals to the mystery lover and the fairy tale lover in me; it is a dark cautionary tale spurred by chance — or fate, if you prefer, like all the best fairy tales.

Helen Georgesson is nineteen, pregnant, and on a west-bound train with seventeen cents in her purse when she meets Patrice Hazzard. The effervescent Patrice is traveling with her new husband Hugh to meet his family. Although Patrice has everything Helen lacks — money, love, family — she has one thing in common with Helen, she is also with child. The women strike up a fast friendship, and while performing their nightly ablutions in the bathroom compartment on the train, Patrice gives Helen her wedding ring to prevent it from falling into the sink drain, inviting her to try it on. Thus, when a devastating train wreck occurs, killing both Hugh and the true Patrice, Helen is assumed to be Patrice Hazzard. Helen spends several drugged months recuperating, but soon she and her infant son are back on the train, en route to the welcoming arms of the Hazzard family.

Helen suffers a crisis of conscience on the train, hearing a whisper from the tracks:

Clicketty-clack,
Stop and go back,
You still have the time,
Turn and go back.

This is much like the warning Cinderella's prince hears in the lesser known version of that story, wherein the evil stepsisters cut off bits of their feet in order to fit the famous slipper.

Turn and peep, turn and peep,
There's blood within the shoe,
The shoe is too small for her,
The true bride waits for you.

Fortunately for Cinderella, the prince heeded that call. Fortunately for readers, Helen does not. Could this decision affect the chance to live happily ever after?

Cornell Woolrich is one of the early masters of noir fiction with many titles to his credit including "Rear Window." *I Married a Dead Man* is captivating from the start; it is an incredible example of the spare yet illustrious writing that defines the noir genre.

Clare Wilcox
"M" is for Mystery, San Mateo, CA

Part II

For this section of the book, I invited each business to comment on the 100 Favorite Mysteries of the Century list — what it represents, suggestions on how to use it, etc. I also invited stores to submit a list of up to five titles that did not make the final list, but should have. Not everyone chose to participate in this section, and several booksellers combined these assignments into one. At the end of this section, I have included a compilation of additional titles suggested by mystery readers.

Booksellers' essays and lists are arranged alphabetically by store name. You can find more information about these businesses in Part III, beginning on page 143.

— Jim Huang

Alibi Books
Glenview, IL

Five titles that should be on the list:

Hocus by Jan Burke
Irene Kelly's husband has been kidnapped and Irene has three days to do what she's told or he dies.

The Strange Files of Fremont Jones by Dianne Day
Fremont Jones is a wonderful and unique main character whose quirkiness is introduced in this first of the series.

The Cater Street Hangman by Anne Perry
The first in the Thomas and Charlotte Pitt series that makes the Victorian Age come to life.

Sudden Prey by John Sandford
My favorite book in a fantastic series about Minnesota cop

Lucas Davenport.

Under The Beetle's Cellar by Mary Willis Walker
Molly Cates, an investigative reporter, finds herself covering a heart-stopping story: eleven children and one bus driver have been abducted by a religious fanatic.

— Sheri Kraft

Aunt Agatha's
Ann Arbor, MI

Five titles that should be on the list:

The Black Dahlia by James Ellroy
James Ellroy isn't just one of the best crime fiction writers in the world, he is, in my opinion, one of the best writers period. *The Black Dahlia* is a landmark novel, a stunning stylistic and thematic achievment that reinvented the noir genre.

The Hours of the Virgin by Loren D. Estleman
Stylistically, Estleman is a match for Raymond Chandler — in *The Hours of the Virgin* his writing reaches a peak where plot, character development and beautiful writing merge.

Ride the Pink Horse by Dorothy Hughes
A perfect hardboiled novel, set in Santa Fe during the carnival, this neglected classic has all the noir elements, and is written in a beautiful, sparse, yet poetic style.

Pomona Queen by Kem Nunn
Criminally neglected, Nunn is one of the most gifted of the writers who rock the crime fiction foundations, adding a modern vitality and wit to the old noir formulas.

Cop Without a Shield by Lillian O'Donnell
O'Donnell was a ground breaker long before Marcia Muller, Sue Grafton and Sara Paretsky came along — she features a

working female New York City police detective with details of police procedures, fair clues, and a strong and emotionally fascinating central character, Norah Mulcahaney.

— Robin & Jamie Agnew

Black Bird Mysteries
Keedysville, MD

Five titles that should be on the list:

Legwork by Katy Munger
A brand new author whose books keep getting better and better (she has four now) and every single one makes me laugh out loud — even now as I remember them!

I, the Jury by Mickey Spillane
You either love him or hate him but Spillane is one of the great hardboiled writers of the century and this is one of his best.

The Daughter of Time by Josephine Tey
Brat Farrar was good but I am fascinated by the historical characters, the political intrigue and the behind-the-scenes maneuvering. Living so close to Washington, DC, with all the local and national political shenanigans, this book reminds me that "everything old is new again."

Under the Beetle's Cellar by Mary Willis Walker
I think this book was superbly written and perhaps the saddest story I've ever read — the characters and the feelings they evoked stayed with me for days.

Though I Know She Lies by Sara Woods
Woods is truly one of my favorite authors and it was very hard for me to pick one title in her Antony Maitland series; I chose this one because it not only is a wonderful British detective story, it has a particularly nice ending.

— Kathleen Riley

Booked for Murder
Madison, WI

Five titles that should be on the list:

The Labyrinth Makers by Anthony Price
The first in an outstanding mystery/espionage series by British author Price introduces David Audley, who is called in to interpret the contents of a World War II plane discovered in the 1970s.

Death Comes as Epiphany by Sharan Newman
This medieval mystery, set in France in the same time period as the Brother Cadfael mysteries, features a young novice in Heloise's convent who travels to St. Denis, where Abbot Suger is raising funds for his Gothic addition to the church.

Remedy for Treason by Caroline Roe (aka Medora Sale) is a wonderful medieval mystery set in Catalonia immediately following the Black Death.

The Raphael Affair by Iain Pears is a delightful art mystery set in Italy.

Bimbos of the Death Sun by Sharyn McCrumb should delight mystery fans even though it is set at a science fiction convention. It reminds me of mystery conventions I have attended.

— *Mary Helen Becker*

Capital Crimes Mystery Bookstore
Sacramento, CA

Five titles that should be on the list:

Night Dogs by Kent Anderson
This stand-alone describing the horrors a Portland police officer brings to the streets from Vietnam is highly recommended to the 50-year-old gray-haired Harley riders who

116

come in looking for a good book to stick in their saddlebags.

Everybody Dies by Lawrence Block

This book marks the blessed snatching of Matt Scudder from the clutches of near-domesticity as some of his friends, characters we have come to know from earlier books, are killed and Matt takes to the streets with saloon owner Mick Ballou to prevent other deaths.

The Neon Rain by James Lee Burke

This novel eloquently births the character of New Orleans homicide cop Dave Robicheaux in a sympathetic and finely written story about a cop and the many demons he faces.

The Final Detail by Harlan Coben

This is the darkest of the Myron Bolitar series, as he and the demented Win try to help their partner, the lovely ex-wrestler Esperanza, who refuses to defend herself against a murder charge.

Maigret and the Madwoman by Georges Simenon

From Paris to the underbelly of the Riviera, Chief Superintendent Maigret investigates the murder of a tiny octogenarian whose claim that someone was "moving things" about in her apartment was dismissed by the police shortly before her death.

— Joe Morales & Mary Ann McDonald

Clues Unlimited
Tucson, AZ

Chris and I feel that the list is useful and interesting not so much for the specific titles, but for the authors. We can and often do disagree about which is the best book by an author, but nearly always agree on whose work is definitely worth reading. That's why we've added authors rather than titles.

Some authors that didn't make the list but should have:

Susan Isaacs created the American suburban cozy and began the tradition leading to today's feisty fortyish female sleuth.

Carolyn Keene! Surely Nancy Drew has been as important a detective as anyone except perhaps Sherlock, and many women tell us that feisty Nancy was their first introduction to the capable, energetic female sleuth we've grown so fond of in more sophisticated versions.

Georges Simenon. How can anybody possibly leave out Inspector Maigret?

Mickey Spillane. Not one of our favorites, but surely important in the hard-boiled tradition.

Andrew Vachss. A man with a mission, whose books radiate dark, angry energy and give an unflinching view of the evils humans are capable of.

— *Patricia Davis*

Creatures 'n Crooks Bookshoppe
Richmond, VA

Meeting someone who becomes a good friend is always a pleasure; to me, it's even better when I come across an old friend I haven't seen in a long time. The 100 Favorite Mysteries list does both for me.

There are books on this list I read years ago, so long ago that I had forgotten them, but I remember that I enjoyed them and now I want to read them again. Other books, and authors, are new to me and I want to read them just as much. I figure if other IMBA members liked these enough to nominate them to the list, they're bound to be special. If only I had 24 hours a day to do nothing but read!

From a business standpoint, the list is invaluable. What better way could there be to build a core stock of outstanding mystery authors and their best titles? My fellow IMBA members are specialists in this field and their opinions are based on what they like to read, not influenced by trying to promote a certain book for sales. These are truly unbiased choices except, of course, for the fact that we all have our personal favorites.

There's nothing I enjoy more than suggesting a favorite to a customer — it's so much fun knowing I've turned a reader on to an author he hasn't tried before — and this list will help me do that.

— Lelia T. Taylor

Deadly Passions Bookshop
Carmel, IN

I've long believed that mysteries have great restorative powers — that in times of illness or trouble, there are few things better than a good mystery, not only to distract us from the problem at hand, but also to renew our spirit and energy. But I'd never personally put this theory to a test in a big way until 1999, when we were struck by two random calamities: serious illness at home and massive layoffs in the downtown where Deadly Passions Bookshop was then located. Through the months of difficult treatment and of watching stores around us close, I was never far from a good mystery.

As 1999 rolled to a close — as both the medical and business situations plodded towards their conclusions (the former ending well, the latter ending sadly) — the opportunity to look back over a century of great books proved an irresistible distraction. I threw myself into this project, shepherding and prodding IMBA into the creation of this list not just for professional goals but for a simple, personal reason as well: the reassurance and comfort of having these books as part of my life.

This list of 100 features many old friends, and a few that I haven't yet met. There are books on this list for every season, every mood — happy or sad. Mysteries open up new worlds, make us think about other people and places, and confront us with challenges — challenges that we hope we could handle as well as our fictional friends do. And mysteries bring smiles to our faces, in the satisfaction of elegant solutions to impossible problems and of resolutions that are just and fair. Mysteries do indeed have great restorative powers — the best mysteries reach us in so many different ways, intellectual and emotional, and usually all at once. They are steadfast and true companions.

Five titles that should be on the list:

The Whispering Wall by Patricia Carlon
A woman paralyzed by a stroke overhears a murderous plot; unable to speak or move, she must find a way to stop the killers. An old-fashioned, read-at-a-gulp suspense novel from an ingenious Australian author.

Audition for Murder by P.M. Carlson
A production of *Hamlet* is the backdrop for murder. Set in the '60s, this is the first book of a wonderful series that offers a luminous portrait of our recent past and of smart, decent, and caring characters whom we love.

Dupe by Liza Cody
Cody's clean, spare prose and cool tone set her apart from most female private eye writers; she's also the best of the bunch — with well-observed detail and a fine sense of irony. PI Anna Lee is as realistic as fictional private eyes get, and the well-constructed plot is full of twists.

The Tightrope Walker by Dorothy Gilman
A young woman finds a cryptic note inside an old hurdy gurdy warning of imminent murder. Through her quest to uncover the mystery, she finds new strength and resolve in her own life.

The Ax by Donald Westlake
After being laid off, Burke Devore devises a murderous yet ruthlessly logical plan to return to the workforce. In this chilling satire, Westlake's masterpiece, he has perfectly captured the essence of contemporary American corporate practices, and what they mean to real people.

— Jim Huang

I Love a Mystery
Mission, KS

Last fall, while other IMBA members were honing the list of 100 Favorite Mysteries of the Century, I was attending to the millions of details involved in opening my bookstore, I Love a Mystery.

Luckily, I joined IMBA just in time to contribute to this book. When editor Jim Huang told me that I could submit a list of five personal favorite mysteries, I was delighted, since I didn't contribute to the "official" list. Had I but known (that's mystery lingo) what agony awaited me, I might have politely declined.

I have a secret: I have the world's worst memory for plots. At first impression, this might seem to be a serious handicap for a mystery bookseller. Not so. After a lifetime of reading mysteries and many years' experience selling them, I'm acquainted with the work of a lot of authors: their styles, their characters, even their titles. I just don't remember the storylines.

This was a big problem as I tried to compile my list of favorites. A few books that I've enjoyed over the years actually stick in my mind with some plot details intact. Are these are my favorites, simply because they were memorable?

Mostly, I have favorite authors — entire bodies of work. Since I can't remember the plots, how can I put my finger on which of their books I like the best? And how can I possibly limit myself to five authors? As I write this, I still haven't decided on my list of five. Most likely, I'll reach a compromise. Or maybe I'll just put some names in a hat.

As for the list of 100 Favorite Mysteries of the Century, we'll find lots of ways to use the book in the store. Some customers love to read their way through a list. The staff will use it for recommendations. It might even be the basis of a book club. Mostly, though, I can't wait to find out what the other booksellers have to say about those 100 books. I just hope that they include detailed plot summaries.

Five titles that should be on the list:

The Portland Laugher by Earl Emerson
I just picked a title at random, because I love every one of
Emerson's mysteries and my customers do, too.

Anonymous Rex by Eric Garcia
An unconventional choice, but I loved this offbeat noir
mystery about a velociraptor private eye guised as a human,
in a world where dinosaurs never became extinct.

Lonely Hearts by John Harvey
The first Charlie Resnick mystery: police procedurals don't
get any better than this series.

Pictures of Perfection by Reginald Hill
It was a toss-up between this book and *The Wood Beyond*,
either of which illustrates that Mr. Hill is an extremely
sophisticated and versatile writer of police procedurals.

The Daughter of Time by Josephine Tey
After 25 years this mystery still sticks in my mind as the best
I've ever read — and it sparked my enduring interest in
English history.

— Karen Spengler

Kate's Mystery Books
Cambridge, MA

We have created a homey atmosphere in the store, with large
overstuffed chairs and stacks of books within easy reach. We
like people to browse in comfort and have created several
special sections in response to frequent queries from customers.
Frequently you can find customers browsing or conversing
with each other in the "Historical," "Strong Women" or "Malice Domestic" sections.

"Staff Picks" is one of the most popular sections and one that
is constantly changing. One thing we have learned is how many

things have to be taken into consideration when picking a mystery. It isn't always just a certain kind of character, setting or quality of the writing. It can depend on the mood you are in when you are looking. For instance, a book that might appeal to me tonight with the rain pounding on the roof might not even make the cut for a trip to the beach. I don't know how I could say which is my *favorite*.

As a result, we haven't specifically used the 100 Favorites List in the store. All the books on it are good (and we try to stock them as both new and used books) but we know it doesn't necessarily represent all of OUR favorites. Any "best of" list compiled by many people is bound to be a compromise. We aren't embarrassed by any titles on the list, but we didn't want to misrepresent ourselves to our customers, or have to explain why one book is on the list and another not.

What we *did* do in thinking about this list was try to think of people who, through their books or series, influenced the direction of the genre in some way either by expanding on a character, crime or setting or by adding a particular twist to the plotting of the mystery itself. I usually advocated for the beginning of a series whenever possible because I think generally series are more pleasurable when read in order.

— *Kate Mattes*

Five titles that should be on the list:

Every person at my store who contributed to this could come up with a completely different list of five more to add. I have let them each have one. One of the things that we all noticed was how white and male the list was. In some ways, this is understandable given the time period is the whole century. Our list tries to add a couple of fresh new voices, as well as correct some serious omissions.

First Hit of the Season by Jane Dentinger

If Agatha Christie suddenly turned into Noel Coward, this is the book she would have written: a wickedly clever puzzle with great theatrical tidbits, witty dialogue and marvelous characters. (Gilly Parker)

Gravedigger by Joseph Hansen
The best entry in the first series featuring a realistic openly gay detective who ages in real time through the series. Unbelievable that it did not make the list. (Mark Banky)

Blue by Abigail Padgett
Both the title and name of this new lesbian detective, *Blue* is one of the freshest, most original voices I have read in a long time — an interesting plot, complex characters and thoughtfully provocative. (Kate Mattes)

The Face of the Stranger by Anne Perry
Richly steeped in the Victorian era, this novel delivers two mysteries in one — Inspector Monk solves the crime and reclaims his identity in the beginning to another great series. (Charlotte Kingsley)

Slayground by Richard Stark
Likable antihero in an intricately plotted thriller with an extremely tense scene in a closed amusement park — should have been a movie. (Andy Levine & Betty Francis)

Dead Ernest by Alice Tilton (aka Phoebe Atwood Taylor) A screwball New England comedy featuring Shakespeare look-alike Leonidas Witherall that would make Groucho Marx proud. Remember Cannae! (Annalisa Peterson)

Lookin for Books
San Diego, CA

Five titles that should be on the list:
What's a Girl Gotta Do by Sparkle Hayter
This book introduces Robin Hudson, who works in television news, has a cat named Louise Bryant and uses one of the most humorous methods for deterring burglars I have ever

heard of in fiction or real life. The series is a wacky look at life in the big city, and Hayter is a great tour guide.

Double Whammy by Carl Hiaasen
This remains my favorite Hiaasen book to date. There is a scene with Lucas the Dog that had me in hysterics.

Watchers by Dean Koontz
My favorite book of all time. What I liked most about this book was the wonderful hero of the book: a golden retriever. This was also a great coming of age book, with a lot of action and suspense.

Death and the Joyful Woman by Ellis Peters
By the author of the Brother Cadfael series, this series takes place in England, and chronicles the doings of CID Inspector Felse and his wife Bunty and young son Dominic. They are delightful.

The Left Leg by Alice Tilton (aka Phoebe Atwood Taylor)
While I enjoy both of Taylor's series, the Leonidas Witherall series is the funniest, indeed some of the funniest books I have ever read.

— Maggie Mason

"M" is for Mystery
San Mateo, CA

Five titles that should be on the list:
Hitman by Lawrence Block
Immediately engaging for those readers curious about the warm heart beating in a cold-blooded killer.

L.A. Requiem by Robert Crais
This one defines the term "un-put-down-able"!

The Dead Cat Bounce by Sarah Graves

We hand sell this book to a huge variety of readers and they always come back for the sequel.

Death Comes as Epiphany by Sharan Newman
It is a huge pleasure to lose oneself in the twelfth century with Newman's cast of complex and endearing characters.

A Cool Breeze on the Underground by Don Winslow
I've learned more tricks of the trade for private investigation from this book than any other; Neal Carey is the most appealing reluctant PI out there.

— Clare Wilcox

Murder by the Book
Portland, OR

Slightly more than half of the titles on IMBA's list were also included in Murder by the Book's selection of its 100 favorite mysteries of the twentieth century, which we've dubbed "Murder by the Century." In assembling our list, we considered only the sheer joy of the read. But in choosing five titles not in the IMBA list that we most wish were, we considered not only how much we liked each title but also the cumulative weight of each author's work in the mystery field in general and, in particular, whether each developed a distinctive approach not otherwise well represented in the IMBA list and that has broadened or deepened our understanding of the genre.

Here are books by five authors who meet these ideals and have touched our hearts and minds in wondrous, dare we say mysterious, ways:

Breakheart Hill by Thomas H. Cook
Haunting history, a love affair turned destructive, small-town life with all its deadly sins (envy) and blessed virtues (courage), and enough Southern ambiance to swallow you up and melt you down: an absolutely stunning novel and only one among his several suspense masterpieces.

King of the Rainy Country by Nicholas Freeling
Impressionistic, spare prose with a conversational style direct from Dutch policeman Van der Valk to the reader, full of continental flavor (food, politics and social clash) — all context for this cagey tale of two missing persons cases converging in murder.

Point of Impact by Stephen Hunter
A terrific, fresh take on the thriller that introduces long-distance sharpshooter Bob "the Nailer" Swagger, a reclusive war hero who stands accused of assassination and must, literally, fire his way to freedom with the help of a gun-shy FBI agent: a great blend of intrigue and mystery, and there are plenty more!

The Long-Legged Fly by James Sallis
Part-time detective, teacher and writer Lew Griffin renders up his cases — missing persons in this first one — in a distinctive voice, with poetic, elegiac prose about loss and survival and about what it means to be a black man working in New Orleans: there are no better detective novels being written.

Gorky Park by Martin Cruz Smith
Smith's ability to capture vividly a time and place previously unfamiliar to the reader (Moscow in the 1970s) helped launch a wave of mysteries set in exotic locales, but few with Smith's brilliance and intensity.

— Jill Hinckley & Carolyn Lane

Murder by the Book
Houston, TX

Five titles that should be on the list:
The Grass Widow by Teri Holbrook
Holbrook's explorations of women's lives in the contemporary South makes for a stunning crime novel.

Houses of Stone by Barbara Michaels
A perfect blending of feminism and the mystery novel.

Cursed in the Blood by Sharan Newman
A superb historical mystery, with memorable characters and a rich, deeply emotional story that lingers on long after the last page has been turned.

The Face of a Stranger by Anne Perry
The introduction of two compelling characters, William Monk and Hester Latterly, and a tour-de-force of a psychological suspense story.

Catilina's Riddle by Steven Saylor
A truly fine historical novel in one of the best historical mystery series being written today.

— Dean James

Murder on Miami Beach
North Miami Beach, FL

When this idea of The List first came up, I was less than enthused. Why bother putting together a list of the 100 Favorite Mysteries of the Century? It's a lot of work, thinking about it and writing a synopsis. And the big job of compiling everyone's opinions, making the decision what to include, what to exclude — let's face it, what would be the point? And we all have small businesses to run and no time to spend on extras.

And then when the list was first published, I took one look at it and was thoroughly intimidated. There were so many books on the list I hadn't read! I'm a mystery bookseller, this is my vocation, now I would be uncovered as a phony and a failure. I thought I was so well read, and my bubble was burst. I was a sham. Big inferiority complex sets in.

A full third of the list contained books I had never read. And worse — there were a good 10 books on the list I had never even heard of, let alone read. Just think, somewhere one of my fellow mystery booksellers thinks a book I had never even heard of is one of the best mysteries of the century. Talk about missing the boat. Talk about feeling inferior and intimidated.

But we like these lists for the same reason we enjoy reading book reviews. To hear about someone else's opinion and maybe get some suggestions about what we ourselves might like to read. It gives us something to strive for, and goals to set. And another tome to add to our To Be Read pile teetering by the side of the bed. (Ok, there's one next to the couch, too). (And by the dining table.) (And by my desk at the store.)

At Murder on Miami Beach Mystery Bookstore, we have formed a 100 Best Mysteries of the Century Discussion Group which is reading each of these 100 on the list, one a month, and using them as a basis for discussion. It is one of the most satisfying book discussion groups I have ever attended.

And as far as being intimidated by the list for showing my ignorance, I feel much better just thinking of the antithesis. What if you looked at that list and thought, "Oh, yeah, I've read them all." Where is there to go from there?

— Joanne Sinchuk

Mysteries & More Online
Austin, TX

Five titles that should be on the list:
Bucket Nut by Liza Cody
One of the most original characters in mystery fiction — a tough-minded, loud-mouthed, plain-jane-female wrestler who you soon are laughing with and then suddenly you realize you have to cheer for this big, strong woman.

Flying Blind by Max Allas Collins
Nate Heller investigates the Amelia Earhart disappearance and gives a plausible explanation. Collins does a superb job with these meticulous modern historicals.

Shackles by Bill Pronzini

This book stretches the private-eye genre and changed the character of "Nameless" in many ways — we gave a "money-back guarantee" with this book but no one ever wanted their money back after reading it.

A Wasteland of Strangers by Bill Pronzini
Only a handful of mystery writers of today could pull off such a powerful suspense novel with seventeen first person narrations and yet Pronzini never enters the main character's head.

New Orleans Mourning by Julie Smith
The first American female Best Novel winner of the Edgar in something like twenty years — it's a powerful and haunting book.

— Jan Grape

Mysterious Galaxy
San Diego, CA

Five titles that should be on the list:
Jan Burke writes some of the best amateur mysteries out there, and her debut novel introducing reporter Irene Kelly, **Goodnight, Irene**, is no exception. *Goodnight, Irene* was a nominee for the Best First Novel for both the Anthony and the Agatha Awards. Irene's job makes the necessary suspension of disbelief for an amateur series easy, and her personality makes her caring and involvement in police matters believable. Add Burke's adherence to the tradition of crimes of the past bearing fruit in the present, and you have a notable book and series. The whole staff is behind this one.

Comic Caper Master Donald E. Westlake deserves a spot on the list of the Century's Best Mysteries for works like **Don't Ask**, the ultimate Dortmunder novel, which finds his hapless thief not only bungling the job, as usual, but also getting himself kidnapped by his targeted victims. John Archibald Dortmunder, like many of Westlake's characters, is a hard-hitting anti-hero portrayed by the man who writes them best. Patrick Heffernan is Westlake's greatest advocate.

Elizabeth Baldwin points out "nobody writes trash crime like Charles Willeford, with his knack for depicting characters with a seamy underbelly." **Miami Blues** helped Willeford, who started out as a pulp fiction writer some 30 years before, make a name for himself. It was also a contribution to the traditions of the bizarre sub-genre of South Florida crime fiction. *Miami Blues*, with Hoke on the trail of a deranged killer, exemplifies the region's literal and figurative decay.

Linda Tonneson pointed out that Janwillem van de Wetering provided the mystery world with some of the finest European police procedural novels, including **Outsider in Amsterdam**. Van de Wetering's multicultural perspective, stemming from his personal travels, helped inform his series about Adjutant Henk Grijpstra and Sergeant Rinus DeGier with a philosophical edge in addition to the nuts and bolts of police work.

Finally, Maryelizabeth Hart strongly believes that Dana Stabenow and series character Kate Shugak should have earned a spot on the list. The first in the series, **A Cold Day for Murder**, won the Edgar for Best Paperback Original. Stabenow's books ably deal with educating readers about Alaska (which is practically a continuing character), and have great scenes (including sex and flying scenes) which celebrate life in contrast to the murders.

Mystery Loves Company
Baltimore, MD

The IMBA list of 100 Favorite Mysteries of the Century represents the growth, diversity and strength of the mystery genre today. It shows how easy it is as a bookseller or reader to find an exceptionally well-written mystery to suit any taste. My partner, Paige Rose, likes hardboiled and private eyes. I prefer British procedurals, literary mysteries and mysteries by women. All of these sub-genres are represented in IMBA's stellar list. The mysteries also depict many epics, historical periods and settings. Many readers like to escape today's stressful times and relax by reading a mystery written during the twenties in an English country estate, or one written in the fifties set on the mean streets of a Big City. However, many of these mysteries are now, sadly, out of print. We hope that the publishers take note of IMBA's choices and bring back these best mysteries. The list has already provided our customers with many suggestions and provoked much discussion in the store. It also has helped us sell a lot of great mysteries.

— *Kathy Harig*

Poe's Cousin
White Plains, NY

This list has been an intensely personal odyssey for me. It stretches from a photo of a little girl in a velvet dress with a lace collar seated in a chair next to the Christmas tree reading Nancy Drew, to a photo of a mature woman, at least in years, standing in front of a wall of books which bears the name "Poe's Cousin." Following Nancy Drew, I became fascinated by Edgar Allen Poe as a writer and as a distant cousin. Family stories brought this renowned writer to life for me. Ian Fleming's James Bond, the hero of my adolescence, did little to raise my feminist consciousness, yet I remember all his great lines ("Shaken, not stirred" "Bond, James Bond"). Historical novels and medieval history became the focus of my voracious reading.

While raising three sons, I ran out of historical novels and read *The Daughter of Time* by Josephine Tey. The combination of historical research, albeit a bit shaky, and mystery hooked me. A friend gave me all his Agatha Christies and I devoured them along with the rest of Tey, Sayers, Allingham, Marsh, Chesterton, Crispin, Ambler, le Carré, James, and so many, many more. Following my "classic" phase, I discovered hundreds of gifted authors, each of whom suited a particular mood or need in me. While I prepared my list of 100 favorite mysteries for this project, each book evoked a personal memory of its place in my life. Mysteries make me laugh with Joan Hess in Maggody, rage against racism with Chester Himes, learn about the Navaho from Tony Hillerman, relish the emergence of feminism in Grace Monfredo's series, and delight in a Boston-brahmin version of my Baltimore family, thanks to Charlotte MacLeod's outrageous parodies in her Sarah Kelling series. What other genre offers such a breadth and depth of place, time and emotion?

Ian Rankin's brilliant John Rebus novels are a clear example of the mystery novel as the truest literary reflection of any given society at any given time. It is fascinating to approach history through these novels which reflect the thought of the day. I feel honored to be part of the mystery world. It has enriched my life through reading and through friendships with authors, book-sellers and customers. The mystery-reading community is different, I believe, because we open ourselves to new ideas and perspectives. Thank you to all who have welcomed me.

Five titles that should be on the list:

The Judas Pair by Jonathan Gash

The Judas Pair introduces the beguiling saga of Lovejoy, a rogue, occasional forger, womanizer, but, above all, a "divvy" who can intuitively ascertain a genuine antique while engaged in dangerous escapades for often shady clients.

The Maggody Series by Joan Hess

Okay, I have a problem. The Maggody book which is my favorite contains an outhouse scene so outrageous that I laugh every time I think of it, but I can't remember which book it's in. So, my recommendation is to start with *Malice in Maggody* and acquaint yourselves with the bizarre, lovable inhabitants of Maggody, Arkansas.

The Family Vault by Charlotte MacLeod

An hysterical send-up of a Boston brahmin family who discover the ruby-encrusted skeleton of a burlesque queen in the family vault, and an introduction to Sarah Kelling, the series' protagonist and sanest member of the clan.

Set in Darkness by Ian Rankin
John Rebus, the most compelling detective in a current series, is morally challenged when an old enemy appears in the guise of an ally in Rankin's latest and most brilliant exercise in moral ambiguity — a uniquely Scottish guilt-trip encompassing political corruption and the new Parliament, homelessness, gangland rivalry and, as always, death.

Absolution by Murder by Peter Tremayne
A splendid first novel in a series about Celtic versus Roman Christianity in 7th Century Britain, which features Sister Fidelma, an Irish Celtic nun and advocate in the Brehon Court, and Brother Edulf, an English Roman Catholic monk.

— Anne Poe Lehr

The Poisoned Pen, A Mystery Bookstore
Scottsdale, AZ

Five titles that should be on the list:
A Toast to Tomorrow by Manning Coles
My favorite espionage novel of all time based on a great McGuffin — is the Nazi's Berlin chief of police who he thinks he is?

The Name of the Rose by Umberto Eco
Often called the great unread bestseller, it is a crime novel, not a classic mystery, and credited with sparking interest in the whole historical mystery genre.

Rogue Male by Geoffrey Household
A classic example of the chase novel pitting two balanced adversaries.

Malice Aforethought by Francis Iles
A suspense classic. We know the doctor did it, but will he get

away with it?

Accounting for Murder by Emma Lathen
Clever plotting drawing upon knowledge of finance — and human nature. *Murder to Go* is funnier.

I'd also like to say that while the rules demand only one novel per author on the list, I disagree with that title selected in many instances. I prefer Cyril Hare's *Tragedy at Law*, Laurie R. King's *With Child* and Robert Barnard's *A Scandal in Belgravia* to name just a few.

— *Barbara Peters*

The Raven Bookstore
Lawrence, KS

The Raven Bookstore helped in compiling this list of 100 Favorite Mysteries of the twentieth Century partly because it's always fun to try to review what you've read and select the best or most memorable titles, and partly because we are so often asked for great mysteries by our customers, and the list seemed like a terrific baseline to begin with.

We wanted the list to be a balance between classic authors and freshly modern ones. Selecting those classic authors who have stood up well over the years, such as James M. Cain, Christie, Hammett, Sayers and Upfield, wasn't too difficult, but it was hard sometimes to choose which of their titles should be on the list. We hope that our readers will understand that often these authors have other excellent titles, some that actually were favorites of one or another contributor. Among the newer authors represented on the list, choosing the ones that will turn into "classics" was a bit more challenging. Authors like Block, Burke, George, Hillerman, Perez-Reverte, King and Walters seem so very solid and continually interesting, but will their stories and the issues hold up? Mostly I think we felt that that if it's a good story, tightly and compellingly told with believable and lively characters and a setting full of interesting and relevant details, these more modern mysteries can't help but be "baby classics."

We put a flier with this list of 100 Favorites in the hands of our customers whenever we can. They are usually excited to have another source for finding good reading and one that comes from an authoritative source. And looking at the list often leads to suggestions of titles by those authors on the list and to discussions about authors that were not selected. Often customers have suggestions of what should be on the list. Books by Airth, Cross, Furst, Gores, Leon, Watson and Westlake are some that have been mentioned.

A real difficulty is that so many of the titles are now out of print. It may provide business for the used and out of print bookshops, but it's darn frustrating to those of us in the retail book business. Our best hope is that publishers, both large and small, will look at the list and decide to bring back many of those titles that are now unavailable.

We are so glad to have this list now and so are our customers!

Five titles that should be on the list:

Malice Aforethought by Francis Iles
No mystery lover should miss this captivating classic puzzle that details from the very first page the plans of the protagonist (a very respectable doctor) to murder his wife.

Seneca Falls Inheritance by Miriam Grace Monfredo
Weaving very accurate and interesting historical details about the women's suffrage movement of the 1850s into this compelling mystery makes this first of a series a great read.

Gaudy Night by Dorothy L. Sayers
Harriet Vane, without Lord Peter, investigates some odd disturbances within the walls of a women's college at Oxford that gives you a glimpse into the daily lives in that fascinating tradition-rich place.

Maigret and the Little Yellow Dog by Georges Simenon

The dry, almost astringent prose of the classic French mystery writer perfectly suits the story of a small town, a small run-down hotel, a small clue in the mangy yellow dog, and a small but deadly crime.

Outsider in Amsterdam by Janwillem van de Wetering
The author's humorous and richly descriptive writing tells the story of three bright and off-beat Amsterdam cops investigating an odd murder amongst the rich burghers and drifting drug users of that gloriously beautiful city in the 1970s.

— Pat Kehde & Mary Lou Wright

Rue Morgue
Boulder, CO

Five titles that should be on the list:
Rogue Male by Geoffrey Household
The best manhunt book in history, expertly paced, tightly plotted and far surpassing John Buchan's more famous *The Thirty-Nine Steps*.

The Murder of My Aunt by Richard Hull
A wickedly funny English novel whose title can — and should — be taken in two ways.

The Paladin by Brian Garfield
This espionage novel is based on a real character, a 15-year-old English boy who acted as Churchill's personal agent in World War II. If you want to convince a teenage boy that reading is a worthwhile endeavor, this book will do it. He just might form a religion around it.

The Angels Will Not Care by John Straley
Straley has breathed new life into the tired old formula of the private eye novel, making him the finest practitioner of this subgenre of his generation, and the best chronicler of wounded

souls who still manage to see the good in other people and the absurdity of life in general.

Death at The Dog by Joanna Cannan
A brilliant novel of character and detection set in a small English village during the first anxious months of World War II, in which a melancholy young Scotland Yarder investigates the murder of a village tyrant and falls hopelessly in love with the unconventional woman who is his chief suspect.

— Tom & Enid Schantz

Seattle Mystery Bookshop
Seattle, WA

Five titles that should be on the list:
Seattle Mystery Bookshop submitted titles by 33 authors who did not make the final list. Narrowing this down to the five which we most regret is tougher than creating our original list was, but here they are, in alphabetical order:

The Poisoned Chocolates Case by Anthony Berkeley
A dazzling example of the traditional puzzle mystery, with six would-be sleuths presenting their solutions, each more plausible than the one before.

Killing Floor by Lee Child
A first mystery with exceptionally polished writing, which has appealed to an unusually wide range of readers.

True Detective by Max Allan Collins
First in the Nate Heller series, seamlessly interweaving fiction and fact.

The Black Dahlia by James Ellroy
A dark masterpiece of crime and human heartache.

Murder Fantastical by Patricia Moyes
The charming British series with Henry Tibbett of Scotland Yard, and his sensible wife Emmy, is at its most delightful when the Tibbetts encounter the eccentric Mandible family.
— *Bill Farley*

Spenser's Mystery Bookshop
Boston, MA

The choosing of the candidates from the outset was heavily weighted to the more modern examples of the genre, which may be our favorites but which cannot begin to be called the best until we define what we think of as the mystery novel. Our novels today, while finding their way onto the bestseller lists as they never did before, are bulky, peopled by characters with quirks and intricately delineated professions and hobbies. They tend to be entertainments more than they are mysteries, novels which include crimes, not novels of detection.

In many cases what separates a book on the list from one that didn't make it is simply accessibility: a number of the best mysteries were simply not in print long enough to find a following. If the list results in the reprinting of books from among its number, or from among the number of worthy books that didn't quite make the list, we could not hope for a more wonderful result.

Five titles that should be on the list:
In **Outsider in Amsterdam**, Zen-influenced Janwillem van de Wetering introduces his trio of charmingly eccentric cops as, with characteristic ambivalence, they pursue the murderer of a drug-dealer.

Frances Fyfield's wonderfully written first novel **A Question of Guilt** introduces Crown Prosecutor Helen West, whose elegance, sensitivity and moral courage make her one of the most compelling heroines in contemporary crime fiction.

Most of Barbara Paul's mysteries command attention, but **Kill Fee**, featuring a hit man who commits murders in advance of payment — threatening those who benefit from the deaths with complicity if they don't pay up — is nothing less than a tour de force.

Rob Kantner's novels featuring Ben Perkins, Detroit's blue collar private eye, are the equal of anything by Robert B. Parker or John D. MacDonald, but perhaps **The Thousand Yard Stare** owns the most sublime plot development, as Perkins attends his high school reunion only to get caught up in the twenty-five-year-old mystery of a girl's suicide on the eve of graduation.

Any of the wonderful series featuring Judy Bolton, the Hardy Boys, and Nancy Drew which drew so many of us into the world of detection when we were kids, especially **The Hidden Staircase** and **The House on the Cliff**.

— *Kathy Phillips & Andrew Thurnauer*

The Mystery Bookstore
Omaha, NE

What strikes me most about the list is its sheer breadth. We go from the coziest of cozies to the blackest of *noir* to the hardest of hard edged. We cover the century. We even include a couple of books, such as Harper Lee's *To Kill A Mockingbird,* that I wouldn't have considered a mystery on first thought.

The second thing about this list was how little squabbling there was when we created it, especially when you consider the many diverse personalities in our group and that many of us proudly live up to the first name of our organization: Independent. There was so much duplication of authors and titles when the individual lists first started rolling in. But there were also cries of, "Oh, yeah! I'd forgotten about that one!"

I'm looking forward to our book, and I hope it gives you as much pleasure to read it as it as we had in making it.

Five titles that should be on the list:
Silver Pigs by Lindsey Davis
Silver Pigs is the first in my favorite series in the whole wide world, and the series I recommend most to customers with any interest in history.

Grave Designs by Michael Kahn
Bawdy, irreverent and anti-establishment, Kahn manages to teach one or two points of law in each book in the series without hitting you over the head.

Death At Rainy Mountain by Mardi Oakley Medawar
Medawar's Tay Bodal series is many things: historical, humorous yet serious; it presents a completely fresh view of Native American culture.

Stone Angel by Carol O'Connell
Mallory's Oracle is important because it's the first in the series (and this series must be read in order), but *Stone Angel* is the culmination and a sheer emotional bloodbath that left me wrung out and begging for more.

The Daughter Of Time by Josephine Tey
Again, I'm simply disagreeing with title rather than author, but then I majored in history in college which is why I am totally unfit for meaningful employment and own a bookstore instead.

— Kate Birkel

The Stars Our Destination
Evanston, IL

Three titles that should be on the list:
The Caves of Steel by Isaac Asimov
OK, blatantly science fiction, but still one of my favorite mysteries.

The Clairvoyant Countess by Dorothy Gilman
It's the engaging characters more than the psychic connection that made it for me.

The Chinese Gold Murders by Robert Van Gulik
Based on an actual magistrate in 800 AD China, Judge Dee would often solve several unrelated but intertwined cases at a time.

— Alice Bentley

... and, finally, mystery fans everywhere

Since this list was published at the end of 1999, mystery fans have made suggestions of titles that should be on the list. Here are just a few of these titles (by authors not represented elsewhere in this book), suggested by fans during a discussion at Bouchercon 2000, by readers of Internet listserv DorothyL and by visitors to the mysterybooksellers.com discussion board:

The Chinese Parrot by Earl Derr Biggers
In the Last Analysis by Amanda Cross
A Maiden's Grave by Jeffery Deaver
The Silent World of Nicholas Quinn by Colin Dexter
Cosi Fan Tutti by Michael Dibdin
Goldfinger by Ian Fleming
Brighton Rock by Graham Greene
Off Minor by John Harvey
Friday, the Rabbi Slept Late by Harry Kemelman
The Voyage of the Chianti by B.J. Morrison
King Suckerman by George Pelecanos
The Complete Uncle Abner by Melville Davisson Post
Miss Lizzie by Walter Satterthwait
Last Seen Alive by Dorothy Simpson
Sex and Salmonella by Kathleen Taylor
The Department of Dead Ends by Roy Vickers
The Four Just Men by Edgar Wallace

Part III

Booksellers contributing to this book

Businesses are listed here by name. Most open stores will also handle your mail, phone, fax and internet orders, while you can visit many mail order businesses by appointment. Following these alphabetical listings, you will find a full list of all IMBA member businesses, organized geographically.

For the most up-to-date information about IMBA member businesses, visit the IMBA website at:
www.mysterybooksellers.com

A Compleat Mystery Bookshop
7 Commercial Alley • Portsmouth, NH 03801
Phone: 603-430-7553
Email: info@compleatmystery.com
Website: www.compleatmystery.com
Type: Open store
Author covered: Ruth Rendell.

Alibi Books
Carillon Square Shopping Center
1434 Waukegan Rd. • Glenview, IL 60025
Phone: 847-657-7832
Email: info@alibibooks.com
Website: www.alibibooks.com
Type: Open store
Authors covered: Jonathan Kellerman, Thomas Perry. See also Part II.

Aunt Agatha's
213 South 4th Ave. • Ann Arbor, MI 48104
Phone: 734-769-1114

Email: auntagathas@mailexcite.com
Type: Open store
Authors covered: James M. Cain, Celia Fremlin, Elizabeth George, Martha Grimes, Kate Ross. See also Part II, and the cover art.

Black Bird Mysteries
P.O. Box 444 • Keedysville, MD 21756-1222
Phone: 301-432-8781   *Toll-free:* 800-449-7709
Email: info@blackbird-mysteries.com
Website: www.blackbird-mysteries.com
Type: Internet
Authors covered: Christianna Brand, Agatha Christie, Chester Himes, Laurie R. King, Ellery Queen. See also Part II.

Booked for Murder
2701 University Ave. • Madison, WI 53705-3700
Phone: 608-238-2701   *Toll-free:* 800-200-5996
Email: booked4murder@mailbag.com
Website: www.bookedformurder.com
Type: Open store
Authors covered: John Ball, John Buchan, Michael Gilbert. See also Part II.

Capital Crimes Mystery Bookstore
906 Second St. • Sacramento, CA 95814
Phone: 916-441-4798
Email: books@capitalcrimes.com
Website: www.capitalcrimes.com
Type: Open store
Authors covered: Michael Connelly, Dick Francis. See also Part II.

Clues Unlimited
123 S. Eastbourne • Tucson, AZ 85716
Phone: 520-326-8533
Email: clues@azstarnet.com
Website: www.cluesunlimited.com
Type: Open store

Authors covered: Arthur Conan Doyle, Arturo Perez-Reverte. See also Part II.

Creatures 'n Crooks Bookshoppe
9762 Midlothian Turnpike • Richmond, VA 23235
Phone: 804-330-4111   *Toll-free:* 888-533-5303
Email: info@cncbooks.com
Website: www.cncbooks.com
Type: Open store
Authors covered: Daphne du Maurier, Dashiell Hammett, Ross Macdonald, Dorothy L. Sayers, Minette Walters. See also Part II.

Deadly Passions Bookshop
484 East Carmel Dr. #378 • Carmel, IN 46032
Toll-free: 800-643-6737
Email: sales@deadlypassions.com
Website: www.deadlypassions.com
Type: Internet
Authors covered: Robert Crais, Jane Langton, Philip MacDonald, S.J. Rozan. See also Part II.

Grave Matters
Box 32192 • Cincinnati, OH 45232-0192
Phone: 513-242-7527   *Toll-free:* 800-491-3741
Email: books@gravematters.com
Website: www.gravematters.com
Type: Mail order
Author covered: K.C. Constantine.

I Love a Mystery
5460 Martway • Mission, KS 66205
Phone: 913-432-2583   *Toll-free:* 877-474-2583
Email: email@iloveamystery.net
Type: Open store
Author covered: Ngaio Marsh. See also Part II.

Kate's Mystery Books
2211 Mass Ave. • Cambridge, MA 02140-1211
Phone: 617-491-2660

Email: katesmysbks@earthlink.net
Website: www.katesmysterybooks.com
Type: Open store
Authors covered: Charlotte Armstrong, Peter Dickinson, Jack Finney, P.D. James, Sara Paretsky. See also Part II.

Lookin for Books
Box 15804 • San Diego, CA 92175-5804
Phone: 619-287-2299
Email: maggiemary@yahoo.com
Type: Mail order
Authors covered: Janet Evanovich, Elizabeth Peters. See also Part II.

"M" is for Mystery
74 E. Third Ave. • San Mateo, CA 94401
Phone: 650-401-8077   *Toll-free:* 888-405-8077
Email: info@MforMystery.com
Website: www.MforMystery.com
Type: Open store
Author covered: Cornell Woolrich. See also Part II.

Murder by the Book
3210 SE Hawthorne • Portland, OR 97214
Phone: 503-232-9995
Email: books@mbtb.com
Website: www.mbtb.com
Type: Open store
Authors covered: Edmund Crispin, James Crumley, Patricia Highsmith, Scott Turow. See also Part II.

Murder by the Book
2342 Bissonnet • Houston, TX 77005-1512
Phone: 713-524-8597   *Toll-free:* 888-4-AGATHA
Email: murderbk@swbell.net
Website: www.murderbooks.com
Type: Open store
Authors covered: Margery Allingham, Reginald Hill, Margaret Millar. See also Part II.

Murder, Mystery & Mayhem

35167 Grand River • Farmington, MI 48335
Phone: 248-471-7210
Email: MMysteryM@aol.com
Type: Open store
Authors covered: Nancy Atherton, Raymond Chandler, Michael Innes, Walter Mosley.

Murder on Miami Beach

16850 Collins Ave. • North Miami Beach, FL 33160
Phone: 305-956-7770
Email: murdermb@gate.net
Website: www.murderonmiamibeach.com
Type: Open store
Authors covered: Carl Hiaasen, Elmore Leonard, John D. MacDonald. See also Part II.

Mysteries & More Online

11804 Oak Trail • Austin, TX 78753
Phone: 512-837-6768
Email: mystrymore@aol.com
Website: members.aol.com/mysterymore
Type: Internet
Authors covered: Lawrence Block, Tony Hillerman, Marcia Muller. See also Part II.

The Mysterious Bookshop

129 West 56th St. • New York, NY 10019-3808
Phone: 212-765-0900   *Toll-free:* 800-352-2840
Email: MysteriousNY@worldnet.att.net
Website: www.mysteriousbookshop.com
Type: Open store
Authors covered: Thomas Harris, John le Carré.

Mysterious Galaxy

7051 Clairemont Mesa Blvd #302 • San Diego, CA 92111
Phone: 858-268-4747   *Toll-free:* 800-811-4747
Email: mgbooks@mystgalaxy.com
Website: www.mystgalaxy.com
Type: Open store

Authors covered: James Lee Burke, Abigail Padgett. See also Part II.

Mystery Loves Company
1730 Fleet St. • Baltimore, MD 21231-2919
Phone: 410-276-6708   *Toll-free:* 800-538-0042
Email: crosemlc@aol.com
Type: Open store
Authors covered: Faye Kellerman, Ed McBain. See also Part II.

Poe's Cousin
9 Windward Ave. • White Plains, NY 10605-5306
Phone: 914-948-0735
Email: a4poe9@westnet.com
Website: www.poescousin.com
Type: Mail order
Authors covered: Sharyn McCrumb, Janet Neel, Ellis Peters.
See also Part II.

The Poisoned Pen, A Mystery Bookstore
4014 N. Goldwater #101 • Scottsdale, AZ 85251
Phone: 480-947-2974   *Toll-free:* 888-560-9919
Email: sales@poisonedpen.com
Website: www.poisonedpen.com
Type: Open store
Authors covered: Dick Lochte, Charles Todd. See also Part II.

Prime Crime
891 Bank St. • Ottawa, ON K1S 3W4 Canada
Phone: 613-238-2583
Email: mystery@magi.com
Website: www.magi.com/~mystery
Type: Open store
Authors covered: Margaret Maron, Peter Robinson.

The Raven Bookstore
8 East 7th St. • Lawrence, KS 66044-2702
Phone: 785-749-3300   *Toll-free:* 888-712-7339
Email: pkraven@webserf.net
Website: www.ravenbookstore.com

Type: Open store
Authors covered: Eric Ambler, James McClure, Mary Roberts Rinehart, Maj Sjöwall & Per Wahlöö. See also Part II.

Remember the Alibi Mystery Bookstore
8055 West Ave. #101 • San Antonio, TX 78213
Phone: 210-366-2665   *Toll-free:* 888-272-5135
Email: patsy@world-net.net
Website: www.rememberthealibi.com
Type: Open store
Authors covered: Aaron Elkins, Carol O'Connell.

Rue Morgue
PO Box 4119 • Boulder, CO 80306
Phone: 303-443-5757
Type: Mail order
Authors covered: Robert Barnard, Craig Rice, Randy Wayne White. See also Part II.

San Francisco Mystery Bookstore
4175-B 24th St. • San Francisco, CA 94114-3614
Phone: 415-282-7444
Email: sfmybooks@aol.com
Website: members.aol.com/sfmybooks
Type: Open store
Authors covered: Nicholas Blake, Bill Pronzini.

Scotland Yard Books
556 Green Bay Rd. • Winnetka, IL 60093-2221
Phone: 847-446-2214
Type: Open store
Authors covered: Sue Grafton, R.D. Rosen.

Seattle Mystery Bookshop
117 Cherry St. • Seattle, WA 98104-2205
Phone: 206-587-5737
Email: staff@seattlemystery.com
Website: www.seattlemystery.com
Type: Open store
Authors covered: Deborah Crombie, G.M. Ford, Rex Stout,

Arthur Upfield. See also Part II.

Sherlock's Home
7 N. Missouri St. • Liberty, MO 64068
Phone: 816-792-0499
Website: www.sherlockshome.com
Type: Open store
Authors covered: John Dunning, Ross Thomas.

Sleuth of Baker Street
1600 Bayview Ave. • Toronto, ON M4G 3B7 Canada
Phone: 416-483-3111
Email: sleuth@inforamp.net
Type: Open store
Authors covered: Sarah Caudwell, Cyril Hare.

Space-Crime Continuum
92 King St. • Northampton, MA 01060
Phone: 413-584-0994   *Toll-free:* 888-844-8924
Email: books@spacecrime.com
Website: www.spacecrime.com
Type: Open store
Authors covered: Nevada Barr, Harper Lee, Dennis Lehane,
Robert B. Parker.

Spenser's Mystery Bookshop
223 Newbury St. • Boston, MA 02116
Phone: 617-262-0880
Email: spenser1@spensersmysterybooks.com
Website: www.spensersmysterybooks.com
Type: Open store
Authors covered: John Dickson Carr, Caroline Graham, Peter
Lovesey. See also Part II.

The Mystery Bookstore
1422 S. 13th St. • Omaha, NE 68108
Phone: 402-342-7343   *Toll-free:* 888-412-7343
Email: hudunit@radiks.net
Website: www.radiks.net/~mysterybookstore

Type: Open store
Authors covered: Dorothy Cannell. See also Part II.

The Stars Our Destination
705 Main St. • Evanston, IL 60202
Phone: 773-871-2722
Email: stars@sfbooks.com
Website: www.sfbooks.com
Type: Open store
Author covered: Fredric Brown. See also Part II.

Whodunit? Mystery Bookstore
165 Lilac St. • Winnipeg, Manitoba R3M 2S1 Canada
Phone: 204-284-9100   *Toll-free:* 800-468-4216
Email: whodunit@escape.ca
Website: www.whodunitcanada.com
Type: Open store
Author covered: Josephine Tey.

IMBA member businesses

The listings in this section are arranged geographically, alphabetically by state and within state by city. Canadian stores appear after those in the US. Most open stores will also handle your mail, phone, fax and internet orders, and you can visit many mail order businesses by appointment.

The Poisoned Pen,
A Mystery Bookstore
4014 N. Goldwater #101
Scottsdale, AZ 85251
Open store

Clues Unlimited
123 S. Eastbourne
Tucson, AZ 85716
Open store

Capital Crimes
Mystery Bookstore
906 Second St
Sacramento, CA 95814
Open store

Lookin for Books
Box 15804
San Diego, CA 92175-5804
Mail order

Mysterious Galaxy
7051 Clairemont Mesa Blvd
Suite #302
San Diego, CA 92111
Open store

San Francisco Mystery Bookstore
4175-B 24th St
San Francisco, CA 94114-3614
Open store

"M" is for Mystery
74 E. Third Ave
San Mateo, CA 94401
Open store

Mysteries to Die For
2940 Thousand Oaks Blvd
Thousand Oaks, CA 91362-3278
Open store

Mysteries By Mail
PO Box 8515
171 C Brush St
Ukiah, CA 95482
Mail Order

Rue Morgue
PO Box 4119
Boulder, CO 80306
Mail order

High Crimes
946 Pearl St
Boulder, CO 80302
Open store

Book Sleuth Mystery Bookstore
2501 West Colorado Ave Suite 105
Colorado Springs, CO 80904
Open store

Murder By the Book
1574 South Pearl St
Denver, CO 80210-2635
Open store

MysteryBooks
1715 Connecticut Ave NW
Washington, DC 20009-1108
Open store

Snoop Sisters Books
11 Sunset Bay
Belleair, FL 33756
Mail order

Mountain Mysteries
PO Box 14158
Bradenton, FL 34280-4158
Mail order

Murder on Miami Beach
16850 Collins Ave
North Miami Beach, FL 33160
Open store

Something Wicked
816 Church St
Evanston, IL 60201
Open store

The Stars Our Destination
705 Main St
Evanston, IL 60202
Open store

Alibi Books
Carillon Square Shopping Center
1434 Waukegan Rd
Glenview, IL 60025
Open store

The Sly Fox
PO Box 117
123 North Springfield St
Virden, IL 62690
Open store

Scotland Yard Books
556 Green Bay Rd
Winnetka, IL 60093-2221
Open store

Deadly Passions Bookshop
484 East Carmel Dr #378
Carmel, IN 46032
Internet

The Raven Bookstore
8 East 7th St
Lawrence, KS 66044-2702
Open store

I Love a Mystery
5460 Martway
Mission, KS 66205
Open store

Spenser's Mystery Bookshop
223 Newbury St
Boston, MA 02116
Open store

Kate's Mystery Books
2211 Mass Ave
Cambridge, MA 02140-1211
Open store

Space-Crime Continuum
92 King St
Northampton, MA 01060
Open store

Mystery Loves Company
1730 Fleet St
Baltimore, MD 21231-2919
Open store

Black Bird Mysteries
PO Box 444
Keedysville, MD 21756-1222
Internet

Aunt Agatha's
213 South 4th Ave
Ann Arbor, MI 48104
Open store

Murder, Mystery & Mayhem
35167 Grand River
Farmington, MI 48335
Open store

Once Upon A Crime
604 West 26th St
Minneapolis, MN 55405-3303
Open store

Sherlock's Home
7 N. Missouri St
Liberty, MO 64068
Open store

The Mystery Bookstore
1422 S. 13th St
Omaha, NE 68108
Open store

A Compleat Mystery Bookshop
7 Commercial Alley
Portsmouth, NH 03801
Open store

The Cloak and Dagger
349 Nassau St
Princeton, NJ 08540
Open store

CSL Books
PO Box 297
Raritan, NJ 08869
Mail order

The Last Good Book
1074 Drewville Rd
Brewster, NY 10509
Mail Order

The Mysterious Bookshop
129 West 56th St
New York, NY 10019-3808
Open store

Poe's Cousin
9 Windward Ave
White Plains, NY 10605-5306
Mail Order

Grave Matters
Box 32192
Cincinnati, OH 45232-0192
Mail order

Strange Birds Books
PO Box 12639
Norwood, OH 45212
Mail order

Malice the Mystery Bookstore
Bend, OR
Internet

Murder by the Book
3210 SE Hawthorne
Portland, OR 97214
Open store

Mystery Books
916 W. Lancaster Ave
Bryn Mawr, PA 19010
Open store

Mystery Lovers Bookshop
514 Allegheny River Blvd
Oakmont, PA 15139-1648
Open store

Adventures in Crime and Space
609A W. 6th St
Austin, TX 78701
Open store

Mysteries & More Online
11804 Oak Trail
Austin, TX 78753
Internet

Murder by the Book
2342 Bissonnet
Houston, TX 77005-1512
Open store

Remember the Alibi Mystery Bookstore
8055 West Ave. #101
San Antonio, TX 78213
Open store

Creatures 'n Crooks Bookshoppe
9762 Midlothian Turnpike
Richmond, VA 23235
Open store

The Old London Bookshop
Box 922
Bellingham, WA 98227-0922
Mail order

Whodunit? Books
301 E. Fourth Ave
Olympia, WA 98501
Open store

Seattle Mystery Bookshop
117 Cherry St
Seattle, WA 98104-2205
Open store

Booked for Murder
2701 University Ave
Madison, WI 53705-3700
Open store

Mystery One Bookshop
2109 N. Prospect Ave
Milwaukee, WI 53202-1110
Open store

CANADA

Whodunit? Mystery Bookstore
165 Lilac St
Winnipeg, Manitoba R3M 2S1
Open store

Prime Crime
891 Bank St
Ottawa, ON K1S 3W4
Open store

Sleuth of Baker Street
1600 Bayview Ave
Toronto, ON M4G 3B7
Open store

Appendix: Shopping list

Current paperback editions are listed with the publisher, ISBN and price, if available as of September 2001. Prices and availability change constantly. Many IMBA member businesses also sell used books, and can help you find titles not currently in print.

❏ ❏ **Margery Allingham**. *The Tiger in the Smoke*
(Carroll & Graf, 0786707194, $5.95)

❏ ❏ **Eric Ambler**. *A Coffin for Dimitrios*
(Vintage, 0375726713, $11.00)

❏ ❏ **Charlotte Armstrong**. *A Dram of Poison*
(not currently in print)

❏ ❏ **Nancy Atherton**. *Aunt Dimity's Death*
(Penguin, 0140178406, $5.99)

❏ ❏ **John Ball**. *In the Heat of the Night*
(Carroll & Graf, 0786708832, $12.00)

❏ ❏ **Robert Barnard**. *Death by Sheer Torture*
(not currently in print)

❏ ❏ **Nevada Barr**. *Track of the Cat*
(Avon, 0380721643, $6.99)

❏ ❏ **Nicholas Blake**. *The Beast Must Die*
(not currently in print)

❏ ❏ **Lawrence Block**. *When the Sacred Ginmill Closes*
(Avon, 0380728257, $6.50)

❏ ❏ **Christianna Brand**. *Green for Danger*
(Carroll & Graf, 0786703865, $4.95)

❏ ❏ **Fredric Brown**. *The Fabulous Clipjoint*
(not currently in print)

❏ ❏ **John Buchan**. *The Thirty-Nine Steps*
(Dover, 0486282015, $1.50)

❏ ❏ **James Lee Burke**. *Black Cherry Blues*
(Avon, 0380712040, $6.99)

❏ ❏ **James M. Cain**. *The Postman Always Rings Twice*
(Vintage, 0679723250, $9.00)

❏ ❏ **Dorothy Cannell**. *The Thin Woman*
(Bantam, 0553291955, $6.99)

❏ ❏ **John Dickson Carr**. *The Three Coffins*
(not currently in print)

❏ ❏ **Sarah Caudwell**. *Thus Was Adonis Murdered*
(Dell, 0440212316, $5.99)

❏ ❏ **Raymond Chandler**. *The Big Sleep*
(Vintage, 0394758285, $11.00)

❏ ❏ **Agatha Christie**. *The Murder of Roger Ackroyd*
(HarperPaperbacks, 0061002860, $5.99)

❏ ❏ **Michael Connelly**. *The Concrete Blonde*
(St. Martin's, 0312958455, $7.99)

❏ ❏ **K.C. Constantine**. *The Man Who Liked Slow Tomatoes*
(not currently in print)

❏ ❏ **Robert Crais**. *The Monkey's Raincoat*
(Bantam, 0553275852, $6.50)

❏ ❏ **Edmund Crispin**. *The Moving Toyshop*
(Penguin, 0140088172, $6.99)

❏ ❏ **Deborah Crombie**. *Dreaming of the Bones*
(Bantam, 0553579312, $6.50)

❏ ❏ **James Crumley**. *The Last Good Kiss*
(Vintage, 0394759893, $11.00)

❏ ❏ **Peter Dickinson**. *The Yellow Room Conspiracy*
(not currently in print)

❏ ❏ **Arthur Conan Doyle**. *The Hound of the Baskervilles*
(Berkley, 0425104052, $4.50)

❏ ❏ **Daphne du Maurier**. *Rebecca*
(Avon, 0380730405, $14.00)

❏ ❏ **John Dunning**. *Booked to Die*
(Pocket, 0743410653, $6.99)

❏ ❏ **Aaron Elkins**. *Old Bones*
(Mysterious, 0445406879, $6.50)

❏ ❏ **Janet Evanovich**. *One for the Money*
(HarperPaperbacks, 0061009059, $6.99)

❏ ❏ **Jack Finney**. *Time and Again*
(Scribner, 0684801051, $13.00)

❏ ❏ **G.M. Ford**. *Who in Hell Is Wanda Fuca?*
(Avon, 0380727617, $5.99)

❏ ❏ **Dick Francis**. *Whip Hand*
(Jove, 0515125040, $6.99)

❏ ❏ **Celia Fremlin**. *The Hours Before Dawn*
(Academy Chicago, 089733101X, $7.95)

❏ ❏ **Elizabeth George**. *A Great Deliverance*
(Bantam, 0553278029, $7.50)

❏ ❏ **Michael Gilbert**. *Smallbone Deceased*
(not currently in print)

❏ ❏ **Sue Grafton**. *"A" Is For Alibi*
(Bantam, 0553279912, $7.99)

❏ ❏ **Caroline Graham**. *The Killings at Badger's Drift*
(not currently in print)

❏ ❏ **Martha Grimes**. *The Man With a Load of Mischief*
(not currently in print)

❏ ❏ **Dashiell Hammett**. *The Maltese Falcon*
(Vintage, 0679722645, $11.00)

❏ ❏ **Cyril Hare**. *An English Murder*
(not currently in print)

❏ ❏ **Thomas Harris**. *The Silence of the Lambs*
(St. Martin's, 0312924585, $7.99)

❏ ❏ **Carl Hiaasen**. *Tourist Season*
(Warner, 0446343455, $7.50)

❏ ❏ **Patricia Highsmith**. *The Talented Mr. Ripley*
(Vintage, 0679742298, $13.00)

❏ ❏ **Reginald Hill**. *On Beulah Height*
(Dell, 0440225906, $6.50)

❏ ❏ **Tony Hillerman**. *A Thief of Time*
(HarperPaperbacks, 0061000043, $6.99)

❏ ❏ **Chester Himes**. *Cotton Comes to Harlem*
(Vintage, 0394759990, $11.00)

❏ ❏ **Michael Innes**. *Hamlet, Revenge*
(not currently in print)

❏ ❏ **P.D. James**. *An Unsuitable Job for a Woman*
(Scribner, 0743219554, $12.00)

❏ ❏ **Faye Kellerman**. *The Ritual Bath*
(Avon, 0380732661, $6.99)

❏ ❏ **Jonathan Kellerman**. *When the Bough Breaks*
(Bantam, 0553569619, $7.99)

❏ ❏ **Laurie R. King**. *The Beekeeper's Apprentice*
(Bantam, 0553571656, $6.99)

❏ ❏ **Jane Langton**. *Dark Nantucket Noon*
(Penguin, 0140058362, $5.99)

❏ ❏ **John le Carré**. *The Spy Who Came in From The Cold*
(Pocket, 0743442539, $13.95)

❏ ❏ **Harper Lee**. *To Kill a Mockingbird*
(Warner, 0446310786, $6.99)

❏ ❏ **Dennis Lehane**. *Darkness, Take My Hand*
(Avon, 0380726289, $6.99)

❏ ❏ **Elmore Leonard**. *Get Shorty*
(Delta, 0385323980, $9.95)

❏ ❏ **Dick Lochte**. *Sleeping Dog*
(Poisoned Pen, 1890208515, $14.95)

❏ ❏ **Peter Lovesey**. *Rough Cider*
(Soho, 1569472289, $13.00)

❏ ❏ **John D. MacDonald**. *The Deep Blue Good-by*
(Fawcett, 0449223833, $6.99)

❏ ❏ **Philip MacDonald**. *The List of Adrian Messenger*
(not currently in print)

❏ ❏ **Ross Macdonald**. *The Chill*
(Vintage, 0679768076, $11.00)

❏ ❏ **Margaret Maron**. *Bootlegger's Daughter*
(Mysterious, 0446403237, $6.99)

❏ ❏ **Ngaio Marsh**. *Death of a Peer*
(St. Martin's, 0312964277, $5.99)

❏ ❏ **Ed McBain**. *Sadie When She Died*
(Warner, 0446609692, $6.99)

❏ ❏ **James McClure**. *The Sunday Hangman*
(not currently in print)

❏ ❏ **Sharyn McCrumb**. *If Ever I Return, Pretty Peggy-O*
(Ballantine, 0345369068, $6.99)

❏ ❏ **Margaret Millar**. *A Stranger in My Grave*
(not currently in print)

❏ ❏ **Walter Mosley**. *Devil in a Blue Dress*
(Pocket, 0671511424, $6.99)

❏ ❏ **Marcia Muller**. *Edwin of the Iron Shoes*
(Warner, 0445409029, $6.50)

❏ ❏ **Janet Neel**. *Death's Bright Angel*
(not currently in print)

❏ ❏ **Carol O'Connell**. *Mallory's Oracle*
(Jove, 0515116475, $6.99)

❏ ❏ **Abigail Padgett**. *Child of Silence*
(not currently in print)

❏ ❏ **Sara Paretsky**. *Deadlock*
(Dell, 0440213320, $6.99)

❏ ❏ **Robert B. Parker**. *Looking for Rachel Wallace*
(Dell, 0440153166, $7.50)

❏ ❏ **Arturo Perez-Reverte**. *The Club Dumas*
(Vintage, 0679777547, $13.00)

❏ ❏ **Thomas Perry**. *Vanishing Act*
(Ivy, 0804113874, $6.99)

❏ ❏ **Elizabeth Peters**. *Crocodile on the Sandbank*
(Warner, 0445406518, $6.99)

❏ ❏ **Ellis Peters**. *One Corpse Too Many*
(Mysterious, 0446400513, $6.99)

❏ ❏ **Bill Pronzini**. *Blue Lonesome*
(Walker, 0802775616, $8.95)
❏ ❏ **Ellery Queen**. *Cat of Many Tails*
(not currently in print)
❏ ❏ **Ruth Rendell**. *No More Dying Then*
(Vintage, 0375704892, $11.00)
❏ ❏ **Craig Rice**. *The Wrong Murder*
(not currently in print)
❏ ❏ **Mary Roberts Rinehart**. *The Circular Staircase*
(Kensington, 1575661802, $5.50)
❏ ❏ **Peter Robinson**. *Blood at the Root*
(Avon, 0380794764, $5.99)
❏ ❏ **R.D. Rosen**. *Strike Three You're Dead*
(Walker, 0802776086, $8.95)
❏ ❏ **Kate Ross**. *A Broken Vessel*
(Penguin, 0140234535, $6.99)
❏ ❏ **S.J. Rozan**. *Concourse*
(St. Martin's, 0312959443, $5.99)
❏ ❏ **Dorothy L. Sayers**. *Murder Must Advertise*
(HarperPaperbacks, 0061043559, $6.99)
❏ ❏ **Maj Sjöwall & Per Wahlöö**. *The Laughing Policeman*
(Vintage, 0679742239, $11.00)
❏ ❏ **Rex Stout**. *Some Buried Caesar*
(not currently in print)
❏ ❏ **Josephine Tey**. *Brat Farrar*
(Scribner, 0684803852, $11.00)
❏ ❏ **Ross Thomas**. *Chinaman's Chance*
(not currently in print)
❏ ❏ **Charles Todd**. *A Test of Wills*
(Bantam, 055357759X, $5.99)
❏ ❏ **Scott Turow**. *Presumed Innocent*
(Warner, 0446359866, $7.99)
❏ ❏ **Arthur Upfield**. *The Sands of Windee*
(not currently in print)
❏ ❏ **Minette Walters**. *The Ice House*
(St. Martin's, 0312951426, $6.50)
❏ ❏ **Randy Wayne White**. *Sanibel Flats*
(St. Martin's, 0312926022, $6.50)
❏ ❏ **Cornell Woolrich**. *I Married a Dead Man*
(Penguin, 0140234276, $5.99)

About IMBA

The Independent Mystery Booksellers Association is a trade association of businesses wholly or substantially devoted to the sale of mysteries. For more information about IMBA, visit the association's website at **www.mysterybooksellers.com**. On the website, you'll find IMBA's monthly bestseller lists, plus lists of the annual Dilys Award nominees and winners. IMBA presents the Dilys Award to the book "we most enjoyed selling" each year. The website also features a discussion board devoted to this 100 Favorite Mysteries of the Century list.

About the editor

Jim Huang is the proprietor of Deadly Passions Bookshop, an internet/mail order bookshop located in Carmel, Indiana and at **www.deadlypassions.com**. Jim is currently serving as director of the Independent Mystery Booksellers Association. Since 1982, Jim has edited and published The Drood Review, a bimonthly mystery review newsletter.

About Drood Review Books

100 Favorite Mysteries of the Century is A Drood Review Book published by The Crum Creek Press. Drood Review Books is the book publishing affiliate of The Drood Review. For more information about Drood and about Drood Review Books, visit **www.droodreview.com** or write:

The Drood Review
484 East Carmel Drive #378
Carmel, IN 46032